Michelle Douglas has been writing for Mills & Boon since 2007 and believes she has the best job in the world. She lives in a leafy suburb of Newcastle, on Australia's east coast, with her own romantic hero, a house full of dust and books, and an eclectic collection of '60s and '70s vinyl. She loves to hear from readers and can be contacted via her website, michelle-douglas.com.

Also by Michelle Douglas

The Vineyards of Calanetti miniseries

Reunited by a Baby Secret

The Wild Ones miniseries

Her Irresistible Protector
The Rebel and the Heiress

The Redemption of Rico D'Angelo
Road Trip with the Eligible Bachelor
Snowbound Surprise for the Billionaire
The Millionaire and the Maid
A Deal to Mend Their Marriage
An Unlikely Bride for the Billionaire
The Spanish Tycoon's Takeover
Sarah and the Secret Sheikh
A Baby in His In-Tray

Discover more at millsandboon.co.uk.

The Million Pound Marriage Deal

MICHELLE DOUGLAS

MILLS & BOON

First published in Great Britain 2018
by Mills & Boon, an imprint of HarperCollins*Publishers*
1 London Bridge Street, London, SE1 9GF

Large Print edition 2018

© 2018 Michelle Douglas

ISBN: 978-0-263-08315-6

MIX
Paper from
responsible sources
FSC
www.fsc.org   FSC™ C007454

This book is produced from independently certified
FSC™ paper to ensure responsible forest management.
For more information visit www.harpercollins.co.uk/green.

Printed and bound in Great Britain
by CPI Group (UK) Ltd, Croydon, CR0 4YY

In memory of James (Jim) Morris
(23/4/51–21/11/17),
who is sadly missed by all
who knew and loved him.

CHAPTER ONE

A QUICK GLANCE around the Soho restaurant informed Sophie that she'd arrived first—which was unusual.

'And that's a gold star for me,' she murmured under her breath, before sending a smile to the approaching waiter. 'I believe there's a reservation in the name of Trent-Paterson.'

'Certainly, madam.'

He didn't even need to check the reservation book, but led her across the room to a table set in an alcove and screened from the rest of the room by palms. Knowing Will, it was probably the best table in the house. She wondered if this was one of the places where he normally brought his women.

Not that they were *his* women, of course. It was just that there was such a parade of them in and out of his life.

You can't talk.

She bit back a sigh.

The restaurant was upmarket, *of course*, and eschewed modern minimalist lines that were currently in vogue, celebrating instead a colonial décor popular over a century ago. It reminded her of Raffles in Singapore. Minus the heat and humidity. This wasn't the kind of establishment that needed to justify itself. She took a seat.

'Can I get you a drink, madam?'

'Yes, please. A sparkling mineral water would be lovely.'

He blinked before his face became a smooth mask again. Ah…so he recognised her too, huh? She resisted the urge to tease him. *New leaf, remember?*

She glanced through the screen of palms at the rest of the room and shook her head. 'Horrible,' she murmured. Normally she and Will met in the café at the Tate Modern. Where they could stare out at the vista spread before them rather than at each other.

And where occasionally their shoulders would bump. Accidentally, of course—Will would never purposely touch his best friend's little sister. Especially not now Peter was dead. But those accidental moments always made her feel less alone.

'Crazy,' she murmured. 'Also you have to stop talking to yourself like this or someone will overhear.' She thought about that for a moment and then shrugged. 'So what?'

It wasn't like a century ago, when they could've had her committed for such eccentricity. Besides, she'd been called far less savoury things than *crazy* by the press…and her father.

She watched the waiter return with both her mineral water and Will, and missed the Tate Modern's café with its view over a grey city. But today called for more salubrious surroundings. Today was Peter's birthday.

Maybe that was why she felt so claustrophobic amid all this airy, white-shuttered cane and palm expansiveness.

Will couldn't see her as well as she could see him, but she tried not to study him too intently anyway, though the temptation lurked at the edges of her consciousness. As usual her heart-rate picked up speed at the sight of those impossibly broad shoulders, long legs and lean hips. William Trent-Paterson was built along lines that made every woman in the room stand to attention, figuratively speaking. A woman had once told her that she ovulated every single time she clapped eyes on Will.

She tried to ignore all thoughts of ovulation, eggs and procreation. Regardless of what Will looked like she knew that, as usual, his lips would press into a thin line when he saw her.

'Such a shame,' she murmured, because, actually, she really liked him. Still, she'd love to see him run to fat. Just a little bit. Just one flaw—that was all she asked. Maybe then she'd feel on more of an even footing with him.

You might as well ask for the moon.

'Sophie,' he said when he reached her.

As predicted those lips pinched together. So did the skin around his eyes. It was a double shame because he had a nice smile, though she rarely saw it.

'Hello, Will.'

She rose and they gave each other perfunctory pecks on the cheeks, keeping the width of the table between them. A rush of lime and a darker musky note flooded her senses. She pulled back and planted herself in her chair again and tried to ignore the heavy thud-thud of the pulse in her throat.

It was like this *every single time*—the stilted distance and the heart thudding.

She suspected it was because there was no other person on the planet who had loved Peter as much as she had…except for Will.

And her father, but that was too difficult.

Since the viciousness of her parents' separation and subsequent divorce when she was eleven and Peter sixteen—when the only thing her parents were focused on was hurting each other—she and Peter had turned to each other. They'd seemed to realise they had no other family to rely on. She'd done her best to stop him from growing too grave and serious, while he'd done his best to stop her from feeling as if she didn't measure up. She'd looked up to him so much. Had depended on him.

And now he was gone…

She couldn't believe the hole it had left in her life.

It made her think that she and Will should hold each other tight on the occasions they did see each other, take comfort in each other. But it was never like that.

Because Will didn't really like her.

But some strange sense of honour kept them in touch, some respect for Peter they weren't prepared to surrender.

Would he be relieved if she hadn't shown up—if she just stopped turning up for their monthly coffee dates and occasional lunches? Would he feel he'd discharged some unspoken duty to Peter and was now off the hook? The thought made her heart ache. She couldn't stop coming. He was one of her last links to Peter.

And Peter was the only person who had truly loved her for who she was.

She couldn't let that go. She couldn't let Peter go, which meant she couldn't let Will go. And she wanted to tell him she was sorry for that, sorry if that made things difficult for him.

But she didn't. Because it would make him uncomfortable…and she didn't want to do anything that would make him uncomfortable. She'd like to make him smile if she could.

'You look glum.'

That slammed her back to the present. 'Sorry, just feeling a bit wistful for…for what could've been.'

He closed his eyes and pinched the bridge of his nose, and she realised he'd thought she was referring to Peter. *Make things more cheerful.*

She waved to encompass the restaurant. 'I've not been here before.'

He straightened. 'Do you like it?'

'It's lovely,' she said, because she was always on her best behaviour with Will.

Amazingly he laughed. 'You hate it.'

'Well, the fact of the matter is I'm starved. So as long as the food is good, I don't care about anything else.'

Those lips pressed back into a tight line. 'Traditionally you barely touch any of your food.'

'Today I can promise you that I'll clean my plate.' *New leaf.*

He raised a sardonic eyebrow. 'You're planning on ordering the green salad and nothing else?'

She snapped her menu closed. 'I'm having the lamb.'

'Excellent choice, I'll have the same.' He handed the waiter his menu, his eyes not leaving hers. 'How's your father?'

Here began the ritual questions. She pushed down a sigh. Just once she'd like… She pushed that thought down too. 'Triumphant that I've been forced to toe the line and run all of his foreseeable charity events.'

For the moment. Beneath the table she twisted her watch around and around on her wrist. She needed a way to find a lot of money fast. Really fast. And she had no idea how she was going to do it. Her father paid her a generous allowance for acting as his event planner, but it was nowhere near enough to help Carla in any practical way…to make amends to the other woman. And she wasn't stupid enough to ask her father for a loan. He'd take too much delight in telling her that she was a carbon copy of her mother and to go to blazes.

Dark eyes surveyed her across the table. 'That's nobody's fault but your own.'

True, but… 'A more gallant man would've refrained from pointing that out.'

'I don't feel like being gallant today, Sophie. I feel like smashing something.'

Her ears perked up. Wow, that was out of character. *Interesting.*

But then he shook himself and asked, 'How's Carla?'

Her appetite fled at the mention of Peter's fiancée. She stared at the screen of palms rather than at him, pain throbbing in the back of her throat. She'd been toying with her bread knife, but she carefully set it back down, afraid that if she didn't she'd stab herself in the leg. Which was no more than she deserved, but *that* might get her committed. Besides it wouldn't help anyone. She couldn't abscond from responsibility. Not this time.

'That good, huh?'

Carla was in drug rehab—drug rehab Sophie had to try and find the money for—but Carla had sworn her to secrecy and Sophie owed her that much. At the very least. Self-loathing bloomed in her chest. How could she have let things get so out of hand? How could she have been so blind? How could she have let Carla—and Peter—down so spectacularly?

She pressed her hands together to stop them from shaking. 'She can't let the memory of Peter go.'

'And we can?'

The words burst from him, unexpected, and Sophie flinched, throwing up an arm as if to ward off the words.

Silence pounded between them.

Eventually Will cleared his throat. 'I'm sorry.'

She could feel the weight of his gaze, but she didn't want to meet it. She adjusted her cutlery instead. 'It's a valid point,' she squeezed out from a tight throat. 'But it's only been two years.' It was too soon for forgetting...for letting go.

From the corner of her eyes she saw him drag a hand back through dark auburn hair. 'I'm starting to think that us continuing to meet like this isn't doing anybody any good, and that—'

'No!'

Her gaze flew to his, snagged and held.

'Please,' she whispered. To her absolute horror tears slid down her cheeks and she wanted to close her eyes and will the floor to swallow her whole. She hadn't let him see her cry, not since the funeral. In the humiliation of the moment she wanted to get up and walk out of this horrible restaurant, but she had to stop what he was trying to do.

'Please, Will, I'm not ready to give this up.' The thought of it filled her with panic. 'Please don't bring an end to...this. I can't—' She swallowed down a sob. 'I know it's uncomfortable. And I know I'm a trial.'

She'd been a trial to every person in her life. Except Peter. She'd try harder not to be a trial to Will in the future. 'But, you see, you loved him. And I loved him. And remembering that, having proof—' *recognition* '—helps.'

His skin had gone grey and his jaw clenched so hard it made her feel sick.

She mopped at her cheeks. 'Will you excuse me while I go find the ladies'?'

He nodded.

'Will you be here when I get back?'

She held her breath until he gave another hard nod. Without another word she fled to the ladies' room, only giving herself enough time to splash some cold water onto overheated cheeks and to repair her eyeliner. Thank God for waterproof mascara!

'I'm sorry,' she said, sliding into her seat again. Their meal had arrived while she'd been away, and she spread her linen serviette across her lap and lifted her knife and fork. 'Today is always a tough day. I'm sorry that you bore the brunt of my dissatisfaction with it.'

'I'm sorry I wasn't more sensitive.'

He wanted to throttle her. She wasn't sure how she could tell—the hard set of his shoulders maybe combined with the deep burning in his eyes.

'How's Carol Ann?' she asked.

'Fully recovered from her surgery. She loved the set of DVDs you sent her. Though from all accounts the rest of the household are being driven insane.'

That made her grin. Carol Ann was Will's younger sister and the same age as Sophie, but she had Down's syndrome with all of the associated health issues that entailed. Sophie had only met her a few times, but she sent her birthday and Christmas cards...and gifts on the few occasions she'd been hospitalised.

They spoke on the phone. Her last gift had been a DVD box set of musicals. 'I'm glad they've been such a hit. The world needs more *The King and I.*'

He almost smiled so she counted that as an almost win.

'How's your grandfather?'

All signs of humour drained from him and she winced. 'The grapevine informs me that he's been making another push to get you to settle down.'

'Good news travels fast. I supposed you were at Catriona McManus's thirtieth last weekend.'

Nope. She'd given up wild times and painting the town red. She was avoiding parties, other than the ones her father was forcing her to plan, organise and host on his behalf. It was all a part of her turning over a new leaf. But that didn't mean she could avoid the rumour mill completely. 'So it's true, then?'

'This time he's given me an ultimatum.'

A forkful of lamb halted halfway to her mouth. 'What kind of ultimatum?'

'Either I marry within the next twelve months and take over the reins of the estate or he's going to give everything to Harold.'

Harold was Will's weasel of a cousin. Her mind raced. Will didn't need the money—he was a squillionaire in his own right. He'd never shown the least interest in inheriting the estate, but... She lowered her cutlery. 'What about Carol Ann?'

'If Harold inherits there'll be no place for Carol Ann at Ashbarrow Castle.'

But...that was Carol Ann's home! Sophie might not know much about Will's life beyond what Peter had told her, and the odd snippet Will occasionally let slip, but she knew he took his responsibility for Carol Ann seriously. She knew how much he loved her. And she knew Carol Ann's entire sense of security was tied to Ashbarrow Castle. She knew because Will had tried moving her to London to live with him and it had been an absolute disaster. Carol Ann had grieved so hard for her home that she'd fallen ill.

Talk about being in a bind. 'What are you going to do?'

He shook his head, remaining silent.

His earlier out-of-character snark made sudden sense. 'Maybe he's bluffing.'

'Not this time.'

Her stomach clenched. Will's parents' marriage had been fraught, ugly…and in the end they'd destroyed each other. All in the glare of the public spotlight. She'd figured that was why he'd sworn never to marry. *Ever.* She'd never met anyone so against the institution. She rubbed a hand across her chest. No wonder he looked so haunted.

Keep things light, she counselled, because he looked ready to snap and she was one of the burdens weighing him down. She lifted a bite of food to her lips, chewed and swallowed. And then she sent him a grin that made him blink. 'I'd marry you for a million pounds, Will.'

He stared at her for a long moment. 'And what would you do with a million pounds?'

She could see in his eyes what he thought she'd do—fritter it away on clothes and parties. She gave up being polite and leaned her elbows on the table. 'Create a new life for myself. A million pounds would let me turn everything around.' It would pay for Carla's treatment. It would let her get the stables up and running so that when Carla was better she'd have a job to come out to.

He leaned towards her, his eyes oddly intent. 'Specifics, please.'

It was the first time in two years that Will had seen anything approaching Sophie's old spark fire through her.

Every time he saw her she'd lost more weight, had grown paler, had become…less.

He'd taken one look at her today and had wanted to punch something.

But now…

She stared at him with those perfect blue eyes—the only part of her that hadn't faded—and blinked. 'Specifics?'

'How would you *specifically* turn your life around with this hypothetical million pounds?'

Her chin wavered between jutting up and angling down. He found himself holding his breath. Would she explain what she meant… or would she wave it all away with a laugh and descend into inanity as usual?

Her chin remained firmly at a midpoint, and he didn't know what that meant. Mind you, he'd never been brilliant at deciphering what went on in that puzzling head of hers. All he knew was that when Peter had died, he seemed to have taken a part of Sophie with him.

And it now seemed that she was incapable of reclaiming it. Or refused to reclaim it. He wasn't sure which.

He knew only what he'd promised Peter— that he'd keep an eye on Sophie—but today he'd had to face the fact that his and Sophie's lunch and coffee dates were doing her more harm than good.

A hand reached inside his chest and squeezed. He'd made her cry. *Well done!* He'd wanted to ease her pain, not add to it. But then, just for a moment, there'd been that spark. As if she'd had a vision of something better.

He wanted to see that spark again. He wanted to help her reclaim the part of herself she'd lost. He wanted to do it for Peter, because of the promise he'd made. But he wanted to do it for Sophie's sake too.

She speared a bean on the end of her fork—delicately because, whatever else you wanted to say about Sophie, she had an innate grace—and ate it. She'd eaten at least half of her meal so far. That in itself was cause for celebration.

'You really want to know?'

'I really want to know.' He knew he must be coming across as intense, but he couldn't help it.

'Well… The first thing I'd do is get out of the city.'

Why? Because of her father? 'I thought you loved London.'

'I do, but it's not exactly been good for me, has it? For the last two years I've thrown myself into the party scene trying to forget. It hasn't worked. All I've done is drunk too much champagne, had too many indiscreet photos snapped by the press and stumbled so late into my job so many times that they had no choice but *to let me go.*'

Until a month ago she'd worked at an art gallery in the West End.

Her fork made a circle in the air. 'Of course, the upside is all of that has annoyed my father no end, so...'

She and Lord Collingford had always had a fraught relationship. It was worse now that Peter was no longer around to play peacemaker.

'But it needs to stop.' She stabbed another bean. 'Enough is enough.'

Her self-awareness surprised him, though he wasn't sure why. She'd never been stupid just...wilful.

'Where would you go?'

'Cornwall.'

His jaw dropped and for the briefest moment she grinned, as if delighted by his surprise.

That spark definitely lurked in the backs of her eyes. What had brought it back?

'My mother's mother left me a bit of land that borders Bodmin Moor. It's not much…but it has a run-down stables and I thought…' She trailed off with a shrug.

He had to fight the urge to lean in towards her. 'You're riding again?' It had been her enduring passion since he'd met her as a pudgy eleven-year-old.

'I never stopped riding, Will.'

She hadn't?

'After Peter died I thought I should give it up. It felt wrong to still enjoy anything.'

He knew what she meant, but… 'He wouldn't have wanted you to.'

She stared down at her plate. *Please don't cry again.*

A moment later she lifted her chin and sent him a game smile. 'I haven't been riding as much these past couple of years as I normally would. Riding and hangovers don't mix.'

She was choosing riding over hangovers? Excellent choice!

'If I had a million pounds I'd turn those stables into a riding school—an equestrian centre. There are a few acres down there so perhaps I could offer agistment as well.'

'How many acres?'

'Seventeen and three quarters. There are fields and a stream but no house.'

Ah.

'My million pounds would buy me a modest cottage.'

It would buy more than that if she had a fancy for grander living, but before she could make any of that a reality, she'd need start-up funds.

She set about demolishing the rest of her lamb. When she was done—and true to her word she cleaned her plate—she set her cutlery onto the plate at a neat angle and dabbed her lips with her serviette. 'Will, for the last five minutes straight you've been staring at me without saying a word. I can't imagine that watching me eat is that fascinating. I really would prefer it if you simply said what was on your mind.'

Her words made him jerk back in his seat. 'Sorry, I didn't mean to be rude. I was thinking.'

'About?'

'I don't want you to take this the wrong way.' He pushed his plate away and folded his arms on the table in front of him.

She grimaced, but her chin didn't drop. 'Okay.'

'But what makes you think you could stick to this hypothetical plan of yours? I mean, running a stables and riding school isn't precisely glamorous. It's hard work and...'

'And hard work isn't something I've been known for these past couple of years.'

She nodded, evidently not the least offended. And that was what got to him about Sophie. She never reacted the way he expected. She could take criticism on the chin.

Unless it came from her father.

She stared up at the ceiling and wrinkled her nose. 'Needs must, Will. I'm losing myself. Playing the party girl isn't the answer—it's left me feeling hollow…ashamed.'

Whoa! He chose his words carefully. 'I think you're being a little too harsh on yourself.'

'No, you don't.'

He blinked.

'And being my father's hostess with the mostest is shredding what little self-respect I have left.'

He could see that was true, even though he didn't understand it.

She pushed her hair back from her face, pulled it momentarily into a tight ponytail that highlighted the exhausted lines fanning from her eyes, and Will's gut gave a sick kick. Hell, he'd be happy to just give her a million pounds, though he knew her pride would forbid her from accepting it.

'Of course, the million pounds is a pipe dream.' She let her hair go and it fell back down around her shoulders in a blonde cloud. 'But my plan is to get a job in Cornwall and save madly until I can do something with my little property.'

'What kind of job are you looking for?' Was she hoping to land another gallery job? He didn't like her chances.

'Events management. I know to the outside gaze it'd look like I'm just continuing with my party-girl ways. But running an event is very different from attending as a guest. I used to run all the gallery's events. And, even if I say it myself, I have a knack for pulling together a halfway decent party, ball, charity luncheon or any other kind of get-together you'd like to name.'

He sat up straighter. She'd be perfect at it. Lord Collingford demanded the best when he entertained. She not only had a name and experience, she had connections. 'You've really thought about this.'

'Doh!' But she smiled as she said it to soften the sting.

'If you were really willing to marry me for a million pounds, Sophie, how would you see that marriage working?'

It was his turn to have the satisfaction of seeing her jaw drop. The waiter chose that moment to clear their plates. 'Would you like to order dessert or coffee?'

'Chocolate cake,' Sophie said, not taking her eyes off Will. 'Please.'

'And champagne,' Will said, holding her gaze. 'A bottle of your best.'

'I wasn't serious when I said I'd marry you for a million pounds,' she whispered, when the waiter had melted into the background again.

'I know. You were being flippant. But if we were to speak *hypothetically...*' He let the rest of the sentence dangle and watched her mind race behind the perfect blue of her eyes. 'I'd put a million pounds into your bank account... What would I get in return?'

'A million pounds...?'

Her eyes glazed over and he could feel his lips start to lift. 'I believe that was the price you put on it.' A million pounds...and then she could live the life she'd just outlined to him.

She shook herself. 'We're playing hypotheticals?'

He nodded.

'Well, if that were to ever happen…it'd have to be a strictly business arrangement. A paper marriage—no sex, no children, no complications.'

He nodded. So far so good.

'You've never wanted to marry.'

The ugliness of his parents' marriage had cured him of ever wanting to trade in his bachelorhood for the vagaries of matrimony. He wasn't inviting that kind of acrimony and spite into his life. The very thought made him break out into a cold sweat.

'But you'll do just about anything to keep Carol Ann healthy and happy,' she continued.

She knew him better than the women he dated. He should find that reassuring considering the conversation they were having, but he didn't. It took a force of will not to run a finger around the collar of his shirt.

She smiled at the waiter as he brought their champagne and slid her chocolate cake in front of her. 'Thank you.'

The waiter's lips lifted and his eyes lit up. 'You're very welcome, madam.'

That was one of the things Will had always liked about Sophie. She didn't just have impeccable manners, but *genuine* manners. She made people feel valued.

'You'd be in London most of the time and I'd be in Cornwall most of the time, so I don't see any reason why we should even have to live together.'

Better and better.

'If you needed me to host the odd dinner party or event I could certainly do that.'

He didn't entertain often but every now and again business demanded it. And he could see how having a 'wife' at those events could be an advantage. Sophie had a talent for ruffling the waters when she had a mind to, but she had an even greater ability for smoothing them.

'Though I'd expect notice. You couldn't just spring events on me at the last minute.'

That was reasonable. 'And if you want me to attend anything you need only let my PA know and—?'

She shook her head. 'In this hypothetical situation you're giving me a million pounds, Will. Nothing more will be asked of you.'

He frowned. That didn't seem fair somehow.

She ate a huge piece of chocolate cake and then nodded and pointed her dessert fork at him, her tongue sweeping out to check for crumbs, leaving a shine on her bottom lip that made something inside him clench tight.

No! Don't do that. Don't look at Peter's little sister like she's a woman, for God's sake.

'I know how much you value your…*independence.*'

Her words hauled him back, and he glanced at her to find her staring at him expectantly. A frown built through him. It wasn't like her to mince her words. 'What are you driving at?'

She shrugged, almost reluctantly...and as if in resignation. 'I know the thought of being monogamous to one woman fills your little bachelor heart with fear and loathing.'

He stiffened. 'It's not fear. It's just... Why the hell would anyone want to do that?'

Her eyebrows lifted. 'Whatever. What I'm trying to say is that I'm not expecting you to abstain sexually during this hypothetical paper marriage of ours. You could continue to have as many lovers as you wanted. But...'

His heart started to thump. 'But...?'

'You might want to consider being discreet.'

Ah. 'I'd have no intention of making you look like a fool or a stooge, Sophie.'

She dabbed at her lips with a napkin. 'While

that's a relief, it's not really what I was getting at. I'm assuming we'd have to put on a convincing show for your grandfather.'

'Only until we were married. I'd have legally binding contracts drawn up. He could do whatever the hell he wants with his title and money, but the deeds to Ashbarrow Castle would pass to me the moment I married.'

'Well, in that case, once we're *hypothetically* married you can be as indiscreet as you want.'

Would it really not bother her? 'And you?'

'You can be assured of my discretion.'

Her answer left him unsatisfied, though he didn't know why.

'We would have to agree to a minimum duration for this paper marriage too,' she added. 'Eighteen months, perhaps?'

He nodded again.

'As for how we got married, that'd be entirely

up to you—a quickie Vegas wedding, a big London society do, or something in between.'

His lip curled. There'd have to be a wedding. Nothing else would satisfy his grandfather, but he couldn't face the thought of some big society affair. 'Could you face a quiet family affair at Ashbarrow?'

She stared at him, and her soft laugh tripped down his backbone. 'The real question, Will, is can you?'

It didn't fill him with a shred of enthusiasm, but if it meant securing Carol Ann's future…

She folded her arms, her eyes narrowing. 'But I have to ask, *hypothetically speaking*, of course. If you were to embark on this paper marriage for real, why would you choose me? There has to be someone more suitable.'

Sophie might have a certain reputation in the tabloids but… He knew a lot of women— all more than happy to keep him company whenever he wanted—but he wouldn't be able to rely on a single one of them to stick to an agreement like this.

Was he really considering this? His gut churned. Was he crazy? Or was this the answer he'd been searching so desperately for?

He drummed his fingers against the linen tablecloth. Beneath the table his foot began to bounce. 'You know me and you know that I don't want to give up either my freedom or my independence. I know you and what you want—money for a fresh start. We'd go into this arrangement with our eyes wide open. You wouldn't be expecting *a husband* in the real sense of the word. I know you wouldn't ever misconstrue our situation. Besides, you're Peter's little sister and, regardless of anything else, I don't believe you'd try and take advantage of being married to me.'

She folded her arms, her chin angling up. 'Are you sure about that?'

Positive. 'You haven't tried putting your price up to two million pounds, have you? Even though you know I'm considering a more than hypothetical arrangement here.'

She shrugged. 'I don't need two million pounds.'

Exactly.

If he married Sophie, it would secure Carol Ann's future. He recalled those few weeks he'd brought her to London to live with him and acid burned his throat. He'd had such high hopes, but she'd become so distraught. *She'd become so ill.* And he'd been helpless to ease her homesickness and her grief at being torn from her home.

Peter had always felt responsible for Sophie in the same way Will felt responsible for Carol

Ann. And if anything were to happen to Carol Ann…

His hands clenched. He couldn't bear the thought, but it reminded him of all the unspoken promises he'd made to Peter when he'd sworn to keep an eye on Sophie—promises to help her wherever and whenever he could. And here was the perfect opportunity to do exactly that.

'I trust you, Sophie.' And there weren't too many people he did trust.

She pursed her lips. 'I've been in the papers a lot recently—always linked with a different guy. I know how much you hate any kind of tabloid attention.'

'Do you mean to continue appearing in the gossip pages?'

'God no!'

He believed her. 'Which makes it a non-issue.'

She stared at him for a long moment. 'If

you were serious about this, we'd need law-yers to draw up pre-nup agreements. I couldn't take you for anything more than that million pounds.' The blue in her eyes started to dance. 'And you couldn't take my little property in Cornwall.'

'Every word is music to my ears, Sophie.'

He poured out two glasses of champagne, and handed her one before raising the other in the air. 'I'm game if you are.'

CHAPTER TWO

'READY?'

Sophie swung from where she stood in front of a gently crackling fire that was more for show than warmth, and nodded across the room to an unsmiling Will. 'Absolutely.'

It was only four days since their crazy lunch in Soho, four days in which they'd signed their names to a contract to seal this crazy deal. Four days in which to consider pulling out.

She pushed her shoulders back. It might be crazy but she wasn't pulling out. All she needed to do to send determination rippling out to every near and far-flung part of her being was to think of Carla. They *would* make this work.

She glanced at Will again. He made no move to lead her downstairs.

They'd been given a suite at the castle—two bedrooms with a shared sitting room and bathroom. It had taken her less time to freshen up than it had him. Which indicated his enthusiasm for the task at hand. She clapped her hands together and tried to look not terrified. 'Ready whenever you are.'

The housekeeper had ushered them to these rooms when they'd arrived. Lord Bramley had not greeted his grandson at the door. Nor had Carol Ann.

If either event had disconcerted or disappointed Will, he'd not betrayed the fact by so much as a flicker of an eyelash.

He ran a critical eye over her now, raising gooseflesh on her arms. 'You look perfect.'

Her lips twisted. She did.

His eyes narrowed. 'What?'

'If there's one thing I *can* do right it's to wear the appropriate clothes whatever the occasion.' And when one got right down to it, it was an utterly pointless talent—so trivial.

She wore black three-quarter-length capris, a silk vest top in cream and a cashmere blend long-line cardigan in a shade of dusky pink. Complementing the outfit was a pair of pink and rose-gold sandals, light make-up and a loose ponytail. She didn't need to glance into the mirror above the mantelpiece to know she looked the epitome of casual country chic.

'What are you afraid you *can't* do? Pull this charade of ours off?'

He wore a pair of navy chinos, loafers and a lighter blue button-down shirt that moulded itself to his chest in such a way that it took an enormous amount of effort on her part to not notice. Or, at least, to appear not to notice.

'You look perfect too. We look perfect together.'

'You didn't answer the question.'

No wonder his start-up company was so successful—he was dogged, persistent when he sensed a problem, and, she suspected, ruthless. Not that she had any intention of hiding her current concerns from him. For heaven's sake, the man had promised her a million pounds! She had to do her absolute best here for him. She had no intention of letting him down— for his sake, for her own sake, but mostly for Carla's sake.

And Peter's.

'Sophie?'

'We *look* perfect.' She twisted the ring on the third finger of her left hand, before holding that hand up. 'We have the ring to prove it. But we need to *act* perfect too.'

He lowered himself to the edge of the sofa. 'Explain.'

She remained right where she was, too keyed-up to take a seat. 'Look, everyone is going to assume we're lovers, right? There are certain… intimacies we need to—'

'We're not having sex! We agreed.'

He remained seated, but it felt as if he'd leapt to his feet and stabbed a finger at her. Her heart gave a sick thud. 'Wow! I don't know whether to be offended that you're so repulsed at the thought of sleeping with me or not.'

This time he did shoot to his feet. 'That's not what I meant.'

'Well, it's by the by and totally unimportant for the current conversation. Sex is not the only kind of intimacy couples in love share.' She planted her hands to her hips to hide how awkward she felt. 'Or has that fact passed you by?'

He dismissed that with a single wave of an imperious hand. 'We'll play it by ear—wing it. Make it up as we go along.'

Did he really think that'd work? An unwelcome thought shuffled through her. She wanted to swat it away, but... 'Are you hoping we succeed? Or that we'll fail?'

'What the hell are you talking about?'

She couldn't take his money. Not if this were a farce. She searched his face.

'I want this to work. It *has* to work.' His nostrils flared. 'What is your problem?'

Her *problem* was his absolute lack of enthusiasm for her company. On their flight to Inverness he'd buried himself in paperwork, barely exchanging two words with her. And at the moment it seemed he could barely stand being in the same room with her. It was some kind of Peter hang-up. She recognised it because she had a few of those of her own.

'My *problem* is that you can barely bring yourself to touch me.'

He scowled. 'You're being ridiculous.'

She held out her hand. 'Then hold my hand.'

His scowl deepened but he took her hand. She immediately felt less alone.

Oh, but that scowl!

She tugged him closer and turned him so they could survey their reflections in the mirror above the mantelpiece. 'Now there's a lover-like expression if I ever saw one.'

He tried to smooth his face out and she was seized with a sudden urge to giggle.

'This isn't funny.'

But his eyes lightened as he said it and her smile widened. 'It's hilarious. You're just too tense to admit it. You're always tense when you mention Scotland, so I suppose it only makes sense that you're tense now we're here.'

His eyebrows rose.

'It's true. It's always been true. There'll be reasons for it—good ones, I expect—but I think it'll help our cause somewhat if you pretend that I've helped you to un-tense a little on that front, don't you?'

He stared down at her and it made her aware of their unusual proximity. Her pulse started to race.

'You've really thought about this, haven't you?'

'Of course I have!' His surprise stung. 'You're paying me a ridiculous amount of money to help you pull this off. I mean to do my best.'

His mouth opened and then closed. He blinked, and then something in the line of his jaw softened. 'Thank you.'

She wanted to tug her hand from his. She wanted to bolt across to the other side of the room and put a sofa and coffee table between them. She forced herself to remain where she was. 'Let's save the gratitude for later…when we've managed to pull this off.'

He gave a hard nod. 'Right. So…any other tricks besides holding hands that I should know about?'

His smile eased the chafe in her soul. This was a tense, high-stakes game they were playing. It made sense there'd be nerves, and that her every sense would be on high alert.

Carefully she reclaimed her hand and gestured to the mirror. 'Pretend it's after dinner and we've all adjourned to the drawing room. For a brief moment the two young lovers edge across to the fireplace to exchange a few private lover-like words.'

He grinned, entering into the spirit of things. His head drew down to hers. 'Sophie?'

His breath stirred the hair at her temples and her heart leapt into her throat. 'Yes?'

'You have the most exquisite toenails I have

ever seen. They rival every other toenail in the universe. You should've been a toenail model.'

She glanced down at her toenails, painted a jaunty pink, and wiggled them. 'I had them done with you in mind.'

Her voice shook as she said it, and they both burst into laughter.

'Did we just spoil the effect you were after?'

She shrugged, shaking her head. 'I have no idea, but I'm pretty certain laughter is good, right?'

He smiled down at her, brushed a tendril of hair from her face. 'It's nice to hear you laugh, Sophie.'

Her stomach clenched. She had no right to laugh. She didn't deserve to have fun. She had too much to make amends for. Once she'd made amends maybe then—and only then— would she have *maybe* earned the right to some happiness.

'Hey, where'd you just go?'

Heavens, she needed to keep on track. 'Sorry, I...' She shrugged. 'Sometimes it still seems wrong to be happy when Peter's not here.'

'He wouldn't want you to keep grieving the way you have been.'

Wasn't that the truth?

But it also wasn't what Will meant, and it was none of his concern. He was doing enough for her already. She had to play her part here to perfection, and if that included laughing then she'd laugh.

'Right, next scenario.'

He straightened. 'Okay, hit me with it.'

'We're at a dinner party. There's milling around before and afterwards. We're talking to another couple or maybe two other couples. How do we stand?'

He pursed his lips. 'You were smart to bring this up. If I think of you as Peter's little sister Sophie, then I stand like this.' He moved a step away. 'At a discreet distance where I'd be careful not to invade your personal space.

He'd always been very careful not to do that.

'But when you're Sophie, my bride-to-be, then…' He was silent for a moment and then draped an arm across her shoulders. Staring at their reflection, he frowned. 'Now we just look like great mates.'

She waited for him to work it out. If she were the one doing all the cosying up it would look wrong. She'd look desperate too. Not that she cared what anyone here thought about her. But she did care about that million pounds, so she had to make sure Lord Bramley didn't get suspicious.

'Okay, this is better.'

Will pulled her in closer until she was plastered against his side. She swallowed. Too close. She rested a hand on his chest.

He frowned. 'That could be a bit much.'

She raised an eyebrow. 'You think?'

'I'm not appreciating your sarcasm.'

Yeah, well, maybe she wasn't appreciating how long this was taking for him to get right. It wasn't as if he hadn't had a lot of practice. It wasn't as if he hadn't had a girlfriend before. He'd had a lot of them.

An itch chafed through her, followed by a burn.

He squared them off, his eyes turned towards the mirror rather than her, until his arm rested across her shoulders, the weight of it solid and reassuring while their hips bumped against each other's lightly. 'That's good. And this could be good too.'

He moved her in front of him and wrapped arm about her upper chest, just above her breasts, pulling her back against him. She gritted her teeth.

'Smile, Sophie.'

She met his gaze in the mirror and forced a smile to uncooperative lips. But as she continued to stare at him a ripple of recognition ran though her. This was Will—Peter's best friend—and while he'd never really approved of her, she'd trust him with her life.

'That's better. This is…nice.'

He smiled back at her, but their gazes clung for a few seconds longer than they should have and Sophie found herself pulling free from Will's embrace when what she really wanted to do was snuggle closer.

'Or,' she said, trying to cover her sudden sense of awkwardness, 'we could simply stand close enough that we brush shoulders.' She gestured to the mirror and brushed her arm against his. 'We could link arms or—'

'Hold hands,' he said, enfolding hers in a warm grasp.

'Or link hands,' she added, desperately trying to ignore the warmth flooding her system as she interlocked their fingers.

'Nice,' he agreed before she broke away.

She could feel his gaze like a physical weight as she took a couple of steps away.

'Is everything okay?'

His voice was quiet, measured, concerned. She turned and sent him what she hoped was a smile. 'I've become a firm believer that what we do with our bodies affects us emotionally.'

He widened his stance. 'You're going to need to explain that.'

She moistened suddenly dry lips. 'All of this touching…it's nice.'

He leaned towards her, a frown in his eyes. 'And?'

'I just don't want either one of us getting the wrong idea and imagining that it means something more.'

He reared back as if she'd struck him. 'If you think I can't control myself—'

'I'm not just talking about sex,' she snapped at him. 'I know you think that we can just breeze in and play these parts and that nothing will change and everything will be hunky-dory and…and tickety-boo!'

He raised an eyebrow. 'Hunky-dory?' His voice grew even more incredulous. 'Tickety-boo?'

She glared at him. 'I don't appreciate your sarcasm.'

He paced away from her, paced back. 'Sorry.'

That didn't look like what he really wanted to say.

His lips thinned. 'So can I assume you don't think this is going to be easy?'

'In my experience nothing is ever as easy as we hope it'll be. And despite what you think, we're playing a dangerous game here. I don't want anyone to get hurt.'

His eyes throbbed into hers. 'You're talking about hearts and emotions now?'

She nodded.

He leaned down so they were eye to eye. 'I can assure you that my heart is in absolutely no danger. You should know me better than that.'

Yes, but she was Peter's little sister. And she didn't know how or why, but in his eyes that made her different from other women.

He straightened. 'Are you telling me your heart is in danger?'

'Absolutely not.' Not as long as she remained on her guard. And she had no intention whatsoever of letting her guard slip. 'But what about Carol Ann and your grandfather?' They could become invested in this fake marriage.

He stilled. 'You'll always be Carol Ann's

friend, won't you? You're not going to dump her the moment we get our divorce.'

'Of course not!'

'Then I think she'll be fine. Thank you for considering her well-being. I appreciate it.'

But she noticed he made no mention of his grandfather's well-being. She didn't pursue it. 'Fine. That leads us to the next topic.'

Will stared at her. He wanted away from the cloying heat of the room. Mind you, it had only become cloying in the last few minutes.

'You're supposed to ask me what topic?' she prompted.

'What topic?' he growled.

She sent him a falsely sweet smile that scraped through him like fingernails on a blackboard. 'Kissing.'

He rocked back on his heels. He couldn't help it. He was simply grateful he managed to stop himself from striding from the room altogether.

She glanced away, her lips pressed into a tight white line that still couldn't hide the luscious curve of her bottom lip. A fact he desperately didn't want to notice.

'Did you really think we'd manage to get through this weekend without the odd peck?'

He let the air out of his lungs, slowly. A peck? He could manage that. Her lips twisted as if she'd read that thought in his face and he knew what message he was sending her—that he found her unattractive. And he could tell she was doing her best to try and not let that bother her…hurt her.

Damn it! He needed this weekend to go smoothly. He needed to convince his grandfather that he and Sophie were serious. He tried to bring Carol Ann's face to mind, but it was

Sophie's wounded eyes that kept appearing there instead.

Damn it! Letting her think that he didn't find her attractive provided him with a measure of protection, but a real man wouldn't let her continue operating under the misapprehension, wouldn't let her take the blame for his own weakness. If it were any other woman...

But it wasn't any other woman. It was Sophie.

Will you keep an eye on her? Be there for her if I can't be?

He'd promised Peter.

He slammed his hands to his hips. 'I don't find you unattractive, Sophie.'

She turned from surveying the fire. 'You don't need to pander to my vanity and make excuses or apologise, Will. These things can simply be a matter of taste or chemistry or—'

He held up a hand, holding her gaze. 'You're

lovely…beautiful.' His gut clenched as he said the words.

She pursed her lips, her eyes narrowing. 'But?'

Her chin didn't drop, the light in her eyes didn't fade, and she suddenly appeared indomitable. Where he'd fancied he'd seen fragility, now there was only strength. It made his mouth go dry though he couldn't fully explain why. Except the realisation that what he thought of her physically maybe didn't matter to her one jot. Which was how it should be, of course. But it left him feeling at a distinct disadvantage.

Right, so that's new, is it?

He ignored the sarcastic voice as best he could, and thrust out his jaw. 'But,' he ground out, 'you're different from the women I date. With them I…'

'Scratch an itch and then move on?' she offered when he hesitated.

It was crude but accurate, and everything inside him rebelled at it. 'We have fun, enjoy each other's company.'

'Yes.'

He shifted under the steadiness of her gaze, shoved his hands into his pockets. 'Are you saying it's different for you and the guys you date?'

'No.'

If he'd been hoping to put her on the defensive he'd have been sadly disappointed.

'The itch I've been scratching, though, is grief, and I finally figured out that the partying, the drinking, the dating an endless parade of guys—*having fun and enjoying their company*—hasn't helped.'

He pulled his hands from his pockets and then didn't know what to do with them. He moistened his lips. 'Has it made it worse?'

How could he help?

She made an impatient movement. 'Not worse. It's just…pointless, and not how I want to spend the rest of my life.' She cocked her head to one side. 'I wonder what itch you're scratching? I think it's a big one.'

He realised then that she wasn't judging him. Lots of women did, and found him wanting. Not that he blamed them. He wasn't cut out for commitment and the long haul. But Sophie was simply trying to work him out. Some of the tension that had him wound up tight eased. When you had parents like his, when you watched them do their best to tear each other apart—and succeed—you promised to never let yourself fall into that same trap, to never get embroiled in the same predicament.

But he didn't want to talk about his parents. 'Is it really so incomprehensible for a guy to simply want to keep his freedom, to not want to be tied down?'

One of her shoulders lifted in a graceful shrug.

'What I'm trying to say, Sophie, is that you're not like the women I usually date and that...' He bit back a curse. 'I can't treat you the way I would them.'

She nodded. 'Because I'm Peter's little sister.'

Exactly.

'And I can't treat you like the guys I've been dating.'

'Because I'm Peter's best friend.'

Very slowly she shook her head. 'Because I like you.' Her eyes grew shadowed. 'And because of who you were to Peter—yes, that too. It means I want you as a part of my life for...'

Things inside him clenched up tight. 'For?'

'Forever. Permanently. I know I'm a trial to

you. I know you probably don't even like me all that much.'

What the hell...?

'But it means I don't want to mess things up between us.'

Where had she got that idea—that she thought he didn't like her?

'You're one of the few links I have left to Peter and I can't bear the thought of losing it.'

Her grief went so deep and he intended to do whatever he could to help her over it. 'That's not going to happen.'

'It will if we mess this up. If we lose our heads and forget ourselves…just once…then we're not going to want to see each other again.'

Her words were like a punch to the gut. Because they were true.

'It's what I meant when I said we were playing a dangerous game.' Her eyes flashed. 'If

you found me unattractive that would be—'
She broke off. 'But you don't.'

And he realised then what she'd made explicit but had left unsaid. She didn't find him unattractive either. The knowledge made his blood roar.

Hell.

He ground his back molars together and counted to three, pulled in a breath. 'You have my word that I won't lose my head.'

He would not let her down.

'And you have my word.'

They had to be cautious, circumspect. He couldn't let himself feel too comfortable with her…and yet they both had to cultivate an appearance of tranquillity with each other for outside eyes. She was right. This could be trickier than he'd first envisaged. But not impossible.

Her lips lifted and she rolled her eyes.

'What?'

Before he knew what she was about she'd leaned in, stood on tiptoe and pressed a kiss to his cheek. 'Thank you.'

His heart crashed in his chest. His cheek burned where her lips had touched him.

She eased back, adjusted her cardigan. 'Right. Your turn.'

She was trying to make kissing him as natural as possible, and he had to do the same. 'Believe it or not,' he said, 'it's my pleasure.'

He pressed a kiss to her brow and tried not to notice how soft and warm and vibrant she felt beneath his lips.

She huffed out a laugh. 'Well, in that case I choose to believe it. Right, sit.'

She gestured to the sofa and he took a seat. She came from behind. Her arms slid around his shoulders, making him start.

'You do that downstairs and you'll give the game away.'

He nodded and gritted his teeth. 'Do it again.'

She eased back, walked away and then moved towards him again and bent down to slide just one arm about his shoulders. He rested his hand on her forearm and felt a tiny tremor run through her. He pulled in a measured breath and her scent flooded his senses. 'You smell nice.'

Nice? That's the best you can manage?

She smelled sensational—fruity and warm, like Christmas. Though Christmas was months away.

'It's my body lotion. Frosted cherry. My favourite.'

They broke apart at exactly the same moment. This was exhausting, but he saw the wisdom of it. They needed to give the impression that they were physically comfortable with each other.

When nothing could be further from the truth.

'Your turn.' He waved her to the armchair.

She sat, leaned back, crossed her legs—for all the world as if she were completely at ease.

Time for them to get this over and done with.

Her eyes widened when he braced his hands on the arms of the chair and leant down towards her, effectively locking her in and leaving her nowhere to escape. 'Lips?'

She glanced at his lips and then back into his eyes and nodded. 'Dry lips,' she whispered. 'And we keep it brief.'

Every cell in his body burst to life. He recited, *Peter's sister, Peter's sister, Peter's sister*, over and over in his mind. 'I want to tell you something before we do this,' he murmured, his gaze not dropping from hers.

She swallowed. 'Okay.'

'You're wrong. I like you just fine, Sophie Mitchell.'

Her lips parted as if in shock. He couldn't resist the pull any longer. His mouth lowered to hers, lips brushing lips—light, teasing and nowhere near enough. She stiffened, but then he felt her force herself to relax. And then she leaned forward a fraction and pressed her lips more firmly against his and kissed him back.

Wind roared in his ears. It took all the strength he had to not deepen the kiss, to not engage lips, mouths, tongues and hands.

Biting back a groan, he pulled back to stare into stunned blue eyes. They were a deeper shade of blue than he'd ever seen before.

She pushed him away and launched herself from the chair like a horse from a starter's gate. 'We better keep that to a minimum.'

She was darn right they were keeping that to a minimum!

He'd kiss her cheek, her brow, the top of her head, her hand, but he had every intention of staying as far away from those lips as possible. They were lethal!

CHAPTER THREE

THE MOMENT SOPHIE and Will entered the drawing room, they were greeted with a squeal and a woman with the same dark auburn hair as Will—Carol Ann—launched herself at her brother with a display of such unadulterated joy all Sophie could do was smile.

When had she lost that easy, unselfconscious joy? The answer came swiftly—when she was eleven years old. She glanced at Will and wondered when he'd lost his.

His current delight at seeing Carol Ann, however, was plain to see. He turned his sister towards Sophie. 'You remember Sophie, don't you?'

She'd prepared herself for any number of

scenarios—from cluelessness as to who Sophie might be, suspicion, perhaps jealousy over Will…and even a studied politeness. What she got though was another whoop of joy and smothered by a hug.

'Sophie's my best friend.'

She was?

'We like the same movies.'

'We certainly do.' For one mischievous moment she was tempted to launch into a song from *South Pacific* or *Grease*, but she was aware of the other two people in the room… and she had a feeling they might not appreciate her musical prowess as much as Carol Ann and Will.

Not that Will would necessarily appreciate it either, but he'd appreciate the effort of making Carol Ann happy.

'She sends me the best presents.' She stared

at Sophie expectantly now. 'Did you bring me a present?'

Will's head rocked back. 'Carol Ann, you can't—'

'Of course I did.' Sophie laughed at a thunderstruck Will. Digging into her pocket, she drew out a small velvet box. 'Here you go.'

Carol Ann opened the box and her eyes went wide. 'It's beautiful!'

It was a bracelet of pink and purple crystals, and she'd known Carol Ann would love it.

The other girl danced on the spot. 'Purple for me! Pink for you!' she shouted.

'Not so loud,' Will admonished, though he couldn't hide his smile.

'Put it on me,' Carol Ann demanded.

Will did and Carol Ann rushed to show it to Ms Grant and her grandfather.

'What did she mean about the colours?' Will asked, drawing her further into the room.

'Purple is Carol Ann's favourite colour and pink is mine.'

'How do you know that?'

'She told me.'

Carol Ann swung back to them. 'Because we talk lots and lots on the phone.'

His eyes widened, but he didn't say anything. She'd thought he knew. She'd thought Carol Ann would've told him. She'd never mentioned it to him herself because he'd never raised the topic. So rather than look at Will, Sophie grinned at Carol Ann. 'Because we're best friends.'

The pressure of his fingers on her arm informed her he'd be following this conversation up when they were alone. 'Do you remember Miss Grant?' He gestured to the other woman. 'She came to London with Carol Ann when they visited.'

She did. Esther Grant was Carol Ann's carer.

The two women smiled at each other. 'Of course I do. How's your father doing, Esther?'

'Coming along nicely, thank you, Sophie.'

'He had a hip replacement last month,' she explained to Will.

Will stared at her with narrowed eyes. 'And are you and my grandfather in regular corre-spondence too?'

She turned to the stocky man who surveyed her from the largest armchair she'd ever seen. 'I don't believe Lord Bramley and I have ever met.'

'Grandfather, I'd like you to meet Sophie Mitchell.'

For a moment she thought the older man wasn't going to rise from his chair, that he meant to snub her completely, but eventually he lumbered to his feet and briefly clasped her hand. 'Your reputation precedes you.'

Ouch! She refused to let her chin drop. 'As

does yours.' She meant it in exactly the same way as he did, and had the satisfaction of seeing his eyes widen.

He briefly clasped Will's hand. He wasn't as tall as Will, but he was broader. Without another word he installed himself in his chair again. Flicking a glance at her left hand, he grimaced. 'I don't need to ask why you've decided to grace us with your presence.'

Carol Ann bustled up between them. 'You're here to visit me, aren't you, Will?'

'That's right,' he agreed.

He met Sophie's eyes over the top of Carol Ann's head and she sent him what she hoped was an encouraging smile. It was nice to see him with his sister, but there was no denying the tension that had him coiled up tight.

'And to tell you that Sophie and I are going to get married.'

Carol Ann's eyes widened.

'As long as that's all right with you,' Sophie added.

More squealing and jumping up and down ensued, especially when she realised Sophie wouldn't just be her best friend but also her sister, until Esther broke in and told Carol Ann that it was time for her Zumba dance class at the local community centre.

The room grew quiet when it was only the three of them left. Dark undercurrents she didn't understand swirled about the room.

'So you're not going to congratulate us?' Will finally said, though his tone implied he didn't care one way or the other if his grandfather approved of the match or not, was happy for him or not. It was all she could do not to wince.

The older man's gaze turned to her. 'I noticed you asked Carol Ann's permission, but you didn't ask mine.'

A myriad different retorts sprang to her lips, but she sensed hurt behind the belligerence so she swallowed them all back. She sensed similar retorts on the top of Will's tongue too, but she rested her hand on his arm to keep him from replying.

Will's grandfather glanced at that hand and then back into her face and pursed his lips.

'Carol Ann is a darling,' she said. 'But Will marrying has the potential to impact on her significantly. We didn't want her security to feel threatened.'

He thrust out his jaw. 'What about my security?'

The muscles under her fingers clenched and she tightened her grip. It took a ludicrous amount of willpower not to let her hand explore the intriguing line of that arm further— to test the solidity of the flesh that quivered beneath her touch. 'Forgive me, sir, but you're a man of the world and you don't need molly-coddling. May we sit?'

She needed to sit before her knees gave out. She didn't wait for an answer, but dragged Will to the sofa and all but fell down into it.

The older man grunted but for a moment she swore she detected a flash of humour in those eyes.

She glanced at Will in her peripheral vision. Why didn't he say something? She gave a sur-reptitious nudge to his ribs.

He started. *Not* the reaction she'd been hoping for. It was all she could do not to roll her eyes.

'I take it, Grandfather, that you're in good health?'

That jaw jutted out. 'Fit as a fiddle.'

'In that case, as you're the one who demanded I marry, I'm at a loss to explain your appalling lack of enthusiasm at my announcement.'

Well, *that* was a no-brainer. He obviously had an objection to Will's choice of bride. But would Lord Bramley say as much in front of her?

She really hoped not because if he did she'd be forced to retaliate. But as the two men's gazes locked and clashed it occurred to her that maybe this had nothing to do with her at all.

What on earth was this pair's problem with each other?

She shuffled upright. 'We were hoping to be married here, at Ashbarrow Castle, if that's all right with you, sir.'

Her words broke through the silent battle and they both swung to stare at her. 'When are you planning to marry?' barked Will's grandfather. 'Spring?'

Spring was six months away.

One corner of Will's mouth lifted, but his

eyes remained as cold as chips of ice. 'We're getting married in three weeks.'

'Three weeks!' The older man glared at them, his jaw working. 'That's impossible. There's too much to organise. People will talk!'

'People always talk,' Sophie broke in. 'But when there's no baby in nine months' time they'll realise they were wrong. I'm not pregnant, Lord Bramley.'

'Then why the rush?'

'I believe you're the one who set the timer, *sir.*'

If Will ever used that tone with her she might just shrivel on the spot!

'Then why don't you just go to some hole-and-corner register office?' he spat.

'Because that's not what I want,' Sophie inserted with a confidence she was far from feeling, her best hostess smile in place. She didn't actually know what a hole-and-corner register office might be, or if it even existed, but she caught the tone well enough. Will was going to give her a million pounds. She had to save the situation before Will blew it and told the old man precisely what he could do with his estate.

She refused to let her smile waver. 'I always swore that when I got married it'd be done right.' She'd just never envisaged a marriage like...this. 'I agree that three weeks isn't much time, but it's doable. Which is just as well as it's the timeframe Will has given me.'

Both men stared at her as if she'd grown a second head.

'Four generations of the Trent-Patersons have been married here at the village church. I happen to think it's important for Will to be married from here as well. It's a tradition that should be preserved.'

A different light came into Lord Bramley's

eyes. He leaned back and folded his arms. Sophie held her breath.

'My grandson doesn't think so. He thinks tradition a waste of time.'

Will's hands clenched. 'When tradition is used as an excuse to force someone to do something unprincipled, when it's an excuse for bad behaviour and deceit, then it's empty, worthless and meaningless. And I refuse to have anything to do with it.'

Wow! Will vibrated with barely contained anger. *Damage control.* 'I think we might've just gone off track.'

Beside her, Will swore. She slipped her hand inside his and he gripped it hard. 'The kind of tradition I'm talking about is a nice one. One that I'd be proud to be a part of.'

Will met her gaze and she sent him a smile. He stared at her for two beats and then shook his head and sent her a rueful smile in return.

Squaring his shoulders, he swung back to his grandfather. 'Sophie has her heart set on being married from Ashbarrow. And I want her to have the wedding of her dreams.'

'What does your father think about this?'

Her stomach clenched at Lord Bramley's sly question. 'As soon as I tell him I'll let you know.'

'He'll have his heart set on a London wedding.'

She bit back an inappropriate smile along with an even more inappropriate gurgle of laughter. 'Nonsense. What he has his heart set on is his daughter mending her wicked ways.'

Lord Bramley remained silent for several long moments. 'Very well, you can be married from here on two conditions.'

Will stiffened. 'If I don't like your—'

She dug her fingernails into the back of his hand. 'Which are?'

'That you delay your nuptials for another week. Give me a month to get the place ready.'

She glanced at Will. His lips thinned into a mutinous line. Lips that had touched hers and sent such a jolt through her she still hadn't recovered. *Don't think about that!* 'Will?' she murmured.

The anger in Will's eyes when he turned to her made her heart beat harder. This was more than just being forced to marry her. There was a whole history of anger that existed between the two men.

'It's only a week,' she whispered. 'It doesn't seem unreasonable. And Carol Ann will enjoy helping me with the preparations.'

At the reminder of what they were really doing here, some of the tension bled from his shoulders. Resignation replaced the anger in his eyes. 'Fine, we'll delay the wedding by one week but not a day more.'

She let out a pent-up breath. So far so good.

'My second condition is that your bride-to-be remains here to oversee the preparations.'

She swallowed. She hadn't foreseen that.

'That's out of the question!' Will shot to his feet. 'I want Sophie in London with me. Besides, she has her own life to lead and her own commitments to take care of, and doesn't have the time to be subjected to your whims.'

'She doesn't have the time to plan her own wedding?'

A million pounds...

'She can organise it from London.'

...in exchange for a month of her life.

'I believe Ms Mitchell can speak on her own behalf.'

'Sophie,' she said automatically. 'Please call me Sophie.' She turned to Will. 'I'd like to be personally involved in the preparations for the wedding, Will. I know I could do it all from

London, but I'll be able to troubleshoot more effectively on the spot, make any split-second decisions that are needed.' And she didn't want Lord Bramley springing any nasty surprises on the day. 'But—' she glanced at the older man '—I need to tell my father the news in person, not over the phone.'

He made a few faces but eventually nodded. 'Yes, I can see how that's necessary.'

'He's out of the country at the moment. He returns on Friday, and we were planning on telling him then.'

She thought hard about the commitments she had for the next month. 'I could fly to London on Friday and stay overnight—we can tell my father that evening. I'll have a chance then to pack for a longer stay here and take care of a few bits and bobs at that end too. I'm also organising a charity ball my father is hosting two Saturdays from tomorrow. All the preparations are complete, except for a few finishing touches, which I can take care of from here, but I will need to return to London to host it.'

The older man looked as if he was going to argue.

The sofa cushion rocked as Will lowered himself back down beside her. 'You don't have to do this.'

Oh, she had the distinct feeling that she did. 'I want to.' She glanced at Lord Bramley again. 'It's the best I can manage, I'm afraid.'

He huffed out a breath.

'Also,' she added, 'I have a couple of conditions of my own.' A sly thought made her add, 'Though I expect Will can take care of those for me.'

The older man stiffened. 'I'm still the master of this establishment,' he thundered. 'I'm fully able to provide my guests with whatever amenities are needed.'

Guest or hostage? But she left that unsaid.

'Excellent! Then I'm going to need access to a car while I'm here.'

Shaggy brows lowered. 'What for?'

She raised an eyebrow. 'Have you ever tried to arrange an event like this before? I'm going to need to hire caterers, bar and wait staff, a photographer, as well as someone to do the cake. Not to mention a dress. At this late stage I can't expect all of the people I need to see to come to me personally.'

'We can use my people in London,' Will said.

'Nonsense! We have better people here in Scotland. I'll make sure there's a car available for whenever you need it, my dear.'

My dear? Heavens!

'What else do you need?'

'A horse.'

'What for?'

'To ride. It'll keep me sane.'

He thrust his jaw out. 'You think being ex-iled to the Highlands is going to be that much of an ordeal?'

'I want to look my best in a month's time, Lord Bramley. And that involves getting plenty of fresh air and exercise to balance out all of the sitting indoors and watching musicals that I plan on doing too.' A stiff canter every day would help her maintain her equilibrium and good humour in the face of Lord Bramley's disapproval. She crossed her fingers. At least, she hoped it would.

'He doesn't trust us.' It was the next morn-ing—early—and not even the crisp clean air or the way the sun sparkled on the dew could lift the weight from Will's shoulders. Sophie had been right. This wasn't going to be easy.

'Of course he doesn't.'

Still, Sophie had somehow taken his grandfather from thinly veiled hostility to almost grudging acceptance. Almost, but not quite.

He scowled. 'And I don't trust him.'

'We can't discuss this in front of your grandfather's staff,' she murmured as they approached the stables. 'Too many people make the mistake of treating the staff as if they're invisible, but they're not. I bet the gardeners and stable hands have worked at Ashbarrow for a long time. Which means they'll be loyal to your grandfather.'

Not that he deserved such loyalty.

'We can't give anyone a reason to suspect anything we don't want them to.'

He glanced at her. She never treated staff as if they were invisible.

Did he?

A groom led out two beautiful-looking steeds and Sophie stilled and clasped her hands beneath her chin as she surveyed them. 'Oh!' Her face softened in awe and appreciation and his heart jerked about in his chest. A moment later she'd kicked herself forward to make friends with them, and the vice about his chest eased a fraction.

Magnus, his grandfather's huge grey gelding, had a reputation for being temperamental and he wanted to caution Sophie to be on her guard. But as he watched her with the horses he closed his mouth again. Both horses nuzzled her hands as she crooned to them.

She had a way with horses. She always had.

Not just horses but dogs too.

And last night it was her lap the household cat had decided to curl up on.

Okay, so she had a way with animals in general. He wondered why she didn't have a pet. Mind you, if she crooned to him like that she'd have him eating out of her hand too. He adjusted his stance. Hypothetically speaking, of course.

She sent him a self-conscious smile and he realised he'd been staring.

'You never told me your grandfather kept such a wonderful stable.'

He shrugged. 'You never told me you and Carol Ann were such regular chatterboxes on the phone.'

Idiot. Not in front of the staff.

But she laughed as if he'd amused her. 'It wasn't a secret. I thought you knew. Now I take it you're riding Magnus and I'm riding Annabelle.'

In all honesty she was the better rider, but he was stronger and Magnus needed a strong hand, so he nodded. And then did his best not to notice the finger-itching shape of her backside as he gave her a leg-up into the saddle.

The bay thoroughbred danced under Sophie's

weight, but a few soft words and a pat to her neck quietened her again.

'She has a way with horses, sir,' the groom said with an approving smile.

What was the man's name? The face was familiar but… He shook his head and vaulted into the saddle. 'I'm in trouble if she challenges me to a race.'

'Magnus will see you right, sir,' the groom said with a grin and Will found himself smiling back. He'd initially suggested the ride for Sophie's benefit, but he found himself looking forward to a long canter.

'Which way?' she asked, and the eagerness in her eyes lightened his heart.

He pointed to the top of a low hill. 'We're going up there.'

'I'm dying for a canter.'

Every atom of her suddenly seemed on the boil, and just for a moment it held him spellbound. He moistened dry lips. 'Meet you at the top, then.'

She didn't need any further permission. She turned Annabelle's head in the direction of the hill, moved into a smooth trot until they'd cleared the yard and then broke into a canter.

Magnus immediately chafed to be after them and it was all Will could do to contain the giant horse until they were free of the yard too. He held him back for a few moments longer before letting him have his head. Only pulling him back again when they'd almost drawn level with Sophie and Annabelle.

Sophie moved as one with her steed, as if she were made of air and water and magic. Her hair streamed behind her, wild and free, and his mouth dried as desire pure and fierce speared into him.

Hell!

He could never act on it. He knew that much,

but it would take an act of God for him to drag his gaze from that slim form at the moment—when it was filled with so much life and strength and purpose.

For the last two years he'd been taking her for coffee and/or lunch. He should've been taking her riding!

When they reached the top of the hill, all four of them were breathing hard. With one hand, she lifted her hair from her neck and stared at the vista spread before them. 'Just… Wow. It's stunning.'

It was. He used to love tramping across these hills and fields. Once. The jewel in the estate's crown was the loch that glinted blue and silver in the sunlight below them. The hill on the far side rose steeply, but on this side all was green and gentle and rolling. In another two months, though, this could all be deep under snow.

But it would still be beautiful.

'I had no idea that your grandfather's estate was so...*lovely*.'

She turned to him and her eyes narrowed when they settled on his face. 'Why should that make you frown?' she demanded.

It wasn't the view, but the heat stampeding through his blood that made him frown. 'What was the name of the groom?'

'Colin. Why?'

'I couldn't remember and it was bugging me. Felt like poor form.'

She sucked her bottom lip into her mouth and chewed on it. *Dear God.* 'I wasn't having some sort of passive-aggressive potshot at you when I said people often treat staff as if they're invisible.'

Which only made it worse because he had the sudden uncomfortable feeling that the criticism should've been aimed at him. 'You knew

Miss Grant's name was Esther,' he couldn't help pointing out.

Sophie shrugged. 'She might be an employee, but she's practically a member of the family.'

His gut tightened. 'What's the housekeeper's name?'

'Ruby, but—'

'And the cook's?'

'Alice.'

She'd been here one night! He'd spent his childhood here and yet he couldn't remember Colin's name. He'd let his resentment at his grandfather spill over to innocent parties. It wasn't good enough.

'Hey.'

He turned at her soft admonishment.

'My father's household staff became my surrogate family. They looked after me during my parents' divorce. At a time when I most needed it. Since then it's become a habit to…' She trailed off with a shrug. 'What are the names of your development team at Pyxis Tech?'

Pyxis Tech was the name of his company. They developed supercharged wireless equipment. He blew out a breath. 'Jason, Daniel, Grace, Graham and Phillip.'

'There you go. You know the names of the staff in your own sphere.'

Her words eased some of the burning in his chest. But it did nothing to ease the heat collecting in his veins. He did his best to ignore it. If he did nothing about it—gave it nothing to feed on—then eventually it would dissipate. He gestured towards the loch. 'Would you like to go down?'

'Yes, please.'

'Can we walk and talk or do you need to canter some more?'

Her gaze sharpened as she glanced into his face. 'We'll walk. What's bothering you?'

He loved that she wasted no time getting to the heart of the matter. 'That you're stuck here for a month.' It wasn't fair on her. It might be true that she needed to tone down the partying and drinking, but that didn't mean she should be cut off completely from all entertainment and social interactions. 'I don't trust my grandfather. He's up to something.'

She grimaced. 'I think you're right. Do you have any idea what, though?'

Not yet, but he'd find out. His hands clenched. Magnus tossed his head in disapproval at the sudden tightening of the reins and he forced his grip to relax once again. 'I'm doing what he's asked. Why can't he just be…satisfied?'

'You're doing what he's asked *literally*, but you've not entered into the spirit of the thing.'

That was asking the impossible.

'And you had to know that when he said he wanted you to settle down he had one of the

Strachan girls in mind or Gloria Campbell or Davina McNally.'

His lip curled. 'Never going to happen.' They were all nice women, but...*no way*. He liked his women footloose and fancy-free. He stayed away from women who'd turned their minds to settling down and making babies.

Annabelle took several dancing steps away as if she suddenly wanted to gallop, but Sophie brought her back under control in an instant. 'Instead you presented him with me. And in his eyes I'm not ideal granddaughter-in-law material.'

Why? Because she'd appeared in the society pages a little too often? Because the papers made her sound wild and out of control? He thrust out his jaw. 'You come from good aristocratic stock. I'm told that's important.'

She huffed out a breath. 'That depends on your definition of *good*, now, doesn't it?'

'I suspect he's going to do his best to make you toss in the towel and give up.' Something ugly shuffled through him. 'He might offer you a bribe to not marry me.'

Blue eyes speared to his. That chin came up. 'I will not accept any bribe from your grandfather. You have my word on it. I can take whatever he dishes out. It's only for a month. But if you doubt that...'

As if by silent accord they pulled the horses to a halt. He stared at her and for the first time that morning he felt like smiling. 'When you look like that it's impossible to doubt you.'

Her shoulders unhitched a fraction. 'Good.'

For the last two years she'd seemed so fragile, but he could see now that she had an underlying strength he'd not recognised before.

Just as you haven't noticed your grandfather's staff.

'I think there's something else at play here.'

She moved off and he had to trot to catch up with her. 'What?'

She shot him a veiled glance and bit her lip as she turned to the front again. 'I think your grandfather is using me as bait.'

'For?'

'You.'

He stared at her, at a temporary loss.

'I think he's hoping that, if he keeps me hostage here, you'll be spending a significant portion of the next month at Ashbarrow too.'

'Of course that's what's going to happen,' he exploded, spooking Magnus. It took a concerted effort to get his excited steed back under control. 'I can't leave you stranded out here on your own.'

Her mouth dropped open. 'Of course you can. One million pounds, Will.'

It still wouldn't be fair.

'And I won't be alone. I'll have Carol Ann

and Esther to keep me company. I can ride when I want.'

He'd make certain she could at least do that.

'And I have a wedding to organise. The month will fly.'

'Staying away won't seem very lover-like.'

'No, you can't stay away completely. You'll need to come up for weekends. But you have a company to run. That's a more than valid excuse for spending most of your time in London.'

It still didn't seem fair.

'And speaking of money…'

His ears pricked up. Had they been? And then he shook himself. 'I'll take care of all your expenses while you're here.'

She nodded and bit her lip. He watched the bob of her throat as she swallowed and imagined what it would be like to explore that throat with his lips.

'May I have a portion of my money up front?'

His gut clenched. 'Why?' What would she need money for while she was stuck at Ashbarrow?

Her eyes flashed. 'You don't get the right to ask how I spend the money, Will. I refuse to be answerable to you on the topic. I'm not a child.'

Ice tripped down his spine. 'Sophie, are you in some kind of trouble?'

Would she even tell him if she was?

'Absolutely not.'

'How much of an advance are you asking for?'

'A hundred thousand pounds.'

Acid burned in his stomach. 'Is someone blackmailing you—the press?' Was there some photograph that—?

'Oh, for heaven's sake, Will, I just want to get things started on the place in Cornwall. It'll be my...*carrot*, my reward, for doing a good job here. It'll remind me what I'm working towards if things get tough here.'

It all sounded perfectly reasonable, but some sixth sense told him she was lying. It also told him not to challenge her. Besides, it would be easy enough to check.

And, whatever else he might think, he'd lay ten times that amount on the bet that she wouldn't take the money and run.

'I'll have the money transferred into your account on Monday.'

CHAPTER FOUR

'IT'S GOING TO start raining again any moment. Go back inside.'

It was Sunday night and she and Will were waiting for the car to be brought around to take him to the airport. It would be both warmer and safer inside the house.

But warm and safe weren't the impressions they were after. They were striving for convincing and believable.

She leaned her shoulder into his. 'But that wouldn't be lover-like, now, would it? And we're being watched.'

He stiffened, but she only noticed because they were touching. She silently blessed him for not glancing in the direction of the great hall's front windows. 'What would you like me to do?'

He said it through gritted teeth. If they'd not had that conversation on Friday night she'd have wanted the ground to swallow her whole. But now she knew where that tension came from, and what it indicated. And in some ways that was worse.

And yet in others…

She refused to finish that thought.

'Sophie?'

What they should do, for the purposes of being convincing, was kiss—deeply, desperately, passionately. But that was too dangerous.

'I want you to drag me into the shrubbery there, out of sight of the windows,' she murmured, rising up on tiptoe to wind her arms about his neck.

One of his arms went about her waist, drawing her close to his lean, hard lines, and it was as if he'd knocked the breath from her body. His other hand slid down to caress her backside. Points of light burst behind her eyelids and it was all she could do to contain a whimper of pure, unadulterated need. Those wicked fingers and the press of his palm made her shift restlessly against him. Heat and need surged through her as he lifted her off her feet and whirled her several feet to the right where they were shielded by a rhododendron.

He loosened his grip immediately, but didn't let her go. In the gathering dusk his eyes looked darker than usual and they throbbed with a primal beat she had a feeling it would be best not to decipher.

'What now?' he ground out.

Her breath came hard and sharp. 'We wait until the car comes.'

She sucked her bottom lip into her mouth and sank her teeth into it, chafed it. She did the same to her top lip, before starting on the bottom one again.

His Adam's apple bobbed up and down. Twice. 'What are you doing?'

'I need to look kissed to within an inch of my life.'

She hadn't known his eyes could go any darker. And she could see him thinking the same thing she'd considered earlier—that the real thing would be far more pleasant. But… 'I don't think kissing for real is a good idea.'

That gaze, heavy and persistent, pulled at something low down in her belly. The lids of his eyes had grown heavy—heavy with thoughts it was definitely in her best interests not to translate—and his lips turned sultry. A man shouldn't look sultry. That was a woman's job! And yet her breath jammed in her throat all the same.

He shuffled in closer. 'If we kiss often

enough it's possible that we could get used to it. Inoculate ourselves to its effects.'

She snatched her hands from where they rested on his shoulders, and set about pinching colour into her cheeks with her fingers, pretending his words had no effect on her. 'Or it could simply lead to other things. No complications, remember? We agreed.'

Kissing Will made things inside her...churn. Not physically, but emotionally. It was possible to have sex—satisfying sex too—without one's emotions being engaged. But instinct told her that'd be impossible with Will.

This was aside from Peter, and aside from Carla. It was about self-preservation because falling in love with Will would be an exercise in masochism. She'd done some stupid things in the last two years, but she wasn't doing that.

She rifled her fingers through her hair, ruffling it first one way and then the other. 'Mess up your hair,' she ordered.

He did as she said.

She refused to focus on how divinely rumpled he suddenly looked. 'I can hear the car coming now.'

The scent of musk and citrus invaded her lungs as he leant in closer. 'We'll video conference every night.'

His hands descended to her shoulders squeezing them in a show of solidarity. She really, *really* wished that touch felt brotherly. 'Okay, just send me an email each day, letting me know what time you'll be free.'

'Sophie...'

She glanced up, mouth open to ask him what other instructions he had for her, when his lips swooped down to hers. One big hand cradled the back of her head to prevent her from drawing away as, with deliberate slowness, his tongue explored the outline of her inner lips with a slow deliberation that had her gripping the lapels of his jacket to keep her upright. This was no pretend kiss! It was hard and hot and demanding.

It was madness!

But he didn't stop.

And she gave herself over to it fully. Winding her arms around his neck, she pressed aching breasts against his chest, seeking relief, but it only inflamed her further. She told herself she was simply playing the game, not that she was powerless to control the rush of desire that pulsed into her every atom and tossed her every which way.

She sank her teeth into his lower lip. She should draw blood, remind him they were playing with fire, but she didn't. She lathed the point with her tongue until he pressed her back, taking control of the kiss again as drop-

lets from the disturbed leaves of the rhododendron bush rained on their heads. He kissed her
with such disturbing thoroughness it felt as if
she'd never been kissed before, and she clung
to him, mindless to everything except the sen-
sations pouring into her.

His hand slid upward from her waist, up towards her breasts, as if he meant to take the
weight of one breast in his hand, to test and
caress it, fondle it, until she'd started to scale
greater heights of pleasure. She wanted that.
Desperately. She pressed against him, silently
urging him on, when they were momentarily
spotlighted in car headlights.

They both froze.

Slowly, Will eased away, keeping an arm
about her until she found her balance. 'I'm
sorry. That was stupid.'

She nodded, unable to speak.

'It won't happen again. I promise.'

She nodded again, wishing it were relief rather than disappointment that was her primary emotion.

It will be later, she told herself. She'd work on it until it was.

They walked back to the path.

He lifted her hand and pressed a kiss to her palm, before striding to the car. He chose to sit in the front rather than the back and she suddenly realised the driver was Colin. She sent him a weak smile and a wave.

The car started to move but then skidded to a halt. What on earth…?

Will's door opened and he leapt out and raced back to her. Good God! He wasn't going to kiss her again, was he?

He took her head in his hands when he reached her and lowered his brow to hers. 'You take care of yourself, Sophie. You hear me?'

'I… Yes, of course.'

'The old man is up to something and I don't want…'

'You don't want what?' she prompted when he hesitated.

He eased back to stare into her eyes. 'I don't want you getting hurt.'

The concern in his eyes melted things inside her that had been frozen for far too long, and she found herself absurdly close to tears. 'I'll be careful,' she whispered. 'I'll stay on my guard.'

'Promise me you'll look after yourself.'

He stared down at her as if he really cared.

Of course he cares. You're Peter's little sister.

But she had a feeling that he no longer saw Peter when he looked at her.

Her heart started to pound.

He drew back, a frown furrowing his brow, and she shook herself. 'You need to go. You're going to miss your flight. And, yes, I promise to look after myself.' She crossed her heart.

His gaze lowered to her chest. His gaze darkened and her breath hitched. But then he simply leaned forward and pressed a kiss to her brow and was gone.

Sophie watched the headlights disappear down the drive and only then did she turn back to the castle, enter the great hall and quietly close the door behind her, shutting out the night and the stars. If only she could shut out the confusion and the desire that continued to burn through her.

'A touching farewell.'

She started, pressing a hand to her chest and locating Lord Bramley a third of the way up the grand staircase. 'I wasn't aware we had an audience.'

He hadn't uttered the words with sarcasm,

thank heavens, but it didn't leave her any the wiser to what he was thinking.

'Luckily my grandson was aware of the possibility and absconded with you into the shrubbery to take his leave.'

Heat flamed in her face. She must look a mess! She tried to smooth her hair down, even though *looking a mess* was exactly the effect she'd been aiming for.

She just hadn't realised they'd achieve the result so spectacularly. Or that it would leave her so discombobulated.

The old man stared at her intently and she found herself moving up the stairs, returning that stare. 'Do you always spy on your grandson?'

'Yes.'

She blinked at his frankness. *Wow!* Why?

It wasn't the question she asked. 'Why don't you like me?'

It was his turn to blink. 'It's nothing personal.'

'It feels personal.'

'I'm not convinced you're good for the lad.'

She chewed that over. 'You're referring to my party-girl reputation. You think I'll be a bad influence on Will.'

'I saw what that kind of lifestyle did to his parents.'

Will's parents had been drug-addled rock stars. 'I don't take drugs!' She released a pent-up breath and tried to moderate her voice. 'Only time will convince you that I've changed. I can't imagine anything I say at the moment will carry any weight with you.'

His eyes narrowed, not in suspicion but more…as if he were assessing her. 'You're more forthright than I expected.'

He approved of that at least. That much was evident.

'But I know who you are. I know you and Will have been meeting regularly ever since your brother died.'

She glanced away to stare at the shadows in the hall below.

'I'm sorry. I understand you must still miss him terribly.'

She couldn't look at him. It still hurt so much to talk about Peter in the past tense. 'You have a problem with us finding comfort in each other?'

'Comfort would be grand, but it seems to me there's little comfort to be had there. It seems more about keeping the wound fresh and open. That does Will no good. He deserves to be allowed to move forward with his life. You do too.'

She couldn't move forward until Carla was well again. But...

'You're still haunted, Ms Mitchell.'

She met his gaze then, and her chest clenched when she saw an almost identical reflection of her own pain in the depths of his eyes. His son, Will's father, had died of a drug overdose when Will was only twelve. He'd been a hard-drinking, out-of-control hellraiser. But she bet none of that had stopped Lord Bramley from loving his son, or from feeling he'd somehow failed him.

'It's late,' he said, swinging away. 'Good-night, Ms Mitchell.'

She bit back a sigh. She'd work on getting him to call her Sophie again in the morning. In the meantime she'd ring Carla's rehab facility and tell them to expect the next instalment of money for Carla's treatment this coming week.

'So you survived your first day alone at Ash-barrow?'

That familiar sardonic eyebrow lifted and

the thing that had felt missing and out of sync since he'd driven away yesterday fell into place now, and she instantly felt more at ease. 'I'm not alone. There's Carol Ann, a household of staff, not to mention your grandfather.'

She adjusted the screen of her laptop. 'Who, it probably won't surprise you to learn, was waiting for me when I came inside after we'd said our…farewells last night.'

All was quiet. It was after eleven o'clock and Sophie sat on the sofa in her private sitting room, elbows on knees and chin in hand, as she contemplated Will's image on her laptop where it was perched on the coffee table before her.

He was still heart-stoppingly gorgeous, even though her screen was in desperate need of a clean, but his potency was muted, thank heavens. It was the distance, the knowledge he was hundreds of miles away, and the fact that he appeared so much smaller on her laptop's screen than he was in real life. The fact she couldn't just reach out and touch him. It contained her temptation while at the same time allowing her to indulge in idle games of *What if?* She didn't need to be so careful of inflaming him…or on her guard for him inflaming her.

He straightened, his eyes shifting into that high-alert expression he often wore whenever he spoke about his grandfather. 'What happened?'

'He's worried I'm going to be a bad influence on you.'

The shock on his face made her laugh, and she set about recounting the conversation.

'You think he's still grieving for my father?'

'I'm sure of it.'

'But…' He frowned. 'That was twenty years ago.'

A weight pressed down on her shoulders. 'I

don't think grieving has a timeframe. I can't imagine a time when I'll ever stop missing Peter.'

But she had to make sure her grief stopped hurting other people. Like Carla and Will.

He stared at her for a long moment. 'That's what I am to you, isn't it—just Peter's best friend?'

She lifted her chin from her hands, shifted back. 'You're not *just* anything, Will. You're your own person.'

He didn't look convinced.

She found herself fighting the urge to lean in closer again. 'Do you care what I think of you?'

'I…' He closed his mouth and shrugged.

She wanted desperately to lighten the mood. 'Sure, a part of me continues to see you as Peter's best friend. But there's a big part of me that's increasingly seeing you as a cash cow.'

Her frank irreverence made him throw his head back and laugh, and she called herself an idiot for thinking anything could mute this man's charisma. It reached out now and wrapped itself about her in ever tighter coils. It made her want things. Things she'd forgotten about.

Things she'd forgotten to want in her grief for Peter.

Things she no longer deserved.

She squared her shoulders. 'And you must still see me as Peter's little sister.' It was what their relationship had been established on.

'Is that what you believe?' He shook his head, sobering. 'The thing is, Sophie, I never did see Peter when I looked at you. I only ever saw you for yourself alone.'

'But…' She picked up the laptop and then didn't know what to do with it.

Dark eyes surveyed her steadily. 'But what?'

'Is that true?'

'It is.'

Then…then that meant he truly did like her—for *herself.* She didn't know what to say.

All she knew was that it left her feeling… golden.

For a moment Will barely recognised the face that stared back at him from his tablet. It was as if something had shifted inside Sophie, and it made his lungs cramp, making it impossible to breathe. He'd always thought her pretty, but now she looked…irresistible.

Maybe it was a trick of the light—maybe his screen needed a good clean. Whatever it was, he was glad they were over five hundred miles apart, and that he couldn't act on the impulses raging through his body.

'Now here's something you will probably be interested in knowing.'

She slid from the sofa to the floor as if to draw closer to him, hugging a cushion to her middle. He'd never been jealous of a cushion before. He swallowed. He had to get a grip before he saw her on Friday night. 'What's that?' he managed to get out.

'Your grandfather is planning to announce our upcoming nuptials in some newspaper I've never heard of.'

Announcement? An announcement hadn't even occurred to him! 'What's this newspaper called?'

He choked when she said its name. 'But that's… It's one of those sensationalist tabloids with zero credibility. You know the ones—*I was abducted by aliens... My canary is possessed... Here's a picture of Jesus's face in a piece of toast*. It's the kind of newspaper he'd call a scurrilous rag.'

Her new-found radiance drained out of her and he wanted to punch something.

'I guess he's making no secret about his lack of faith in our marriage, then…in his disapproval of your choice of bride.'

She bit her lip and he noticed how tightly she clutched the cushion to her chest. 'What?' he barked.

'If we can't get him to buy into the validity of our marriage then how are you going to get him to sign Ashbarrow over to you?'

It was a tricky situation, there was no denying that, but he'd been in trickier ones. And he wasn't sure what it said about him, but at the moment he was more interested in seeing her smile than he was in his grandfather. And it occurred to him exactly how to make that happen.

'What?' She shot forward, her eyes wide. 'Tell me what you're planning.'

She had beautiful lips. He'd been an idiot to kiss her last night, but that ridiculous temptation had seized him with a recklessness he'd thought he'd left behind at fourteen years of age. He'd used the excuse of their situation to kiss her deeply and completely. He'd wanted to experience it just once.

And it was all he'd been able to think about since. He burned to do it again.

You can't. This is Sophie. He'd promised no complications. And sex would be a complication. She'd made it clear she didn't want to be one of the parade of women who shared his bed. While he…? He'd give a lot to be one of the men to share her bed.

As long as he kept the thought of those other men out of his mind.

Keep sex and Sophie out of your mind.

Excellent advice. If only he could follow it.

'Oh, my God, Will. You're killing me here. Tell me your plan!'

Those lips… They were a dusky plum and perfectly shaped to fit his and, just from looking, he'd have never known that. But he did now. It made him realise the power of the mythical forbidden fruit.

He had to keep his head. For Sophie's sake. She deserved better from him.

'Will!' She groaned and disappeared, presumably fell on her side in a fever of impatience, and he suddenly found himself laughing. 'Give,' she ordered, popping back into view.

'Tomorrow I'm going to have our engagement announced in every major newspaper in the UK.'

She stared at him, her eyes widened, and then she clapped her hands and threw her head back on a laugh. 'That's…inspired!'

Whatever else it was, it had made her smile, and that was all that mattered. Something inside him lifted.

'So…what's the deal with you and your grandfather?'

He crashed back to earth. It was all he could do not to scowl. 'You know how these things are.' He tried to shrug it off. 'Families.' He uttered the word as if it explained everything. 'Given your relationship with your father, I expect you can empathise.'

She shook her head. '"Every unhappy family is unhappy in its own way."'

The line sounded vaguely familiar and she said it as if quoting from a book. She'd always been a big reader. Him not so much.

'My father and I are unhappy because I look a lot like my mother and he can't see past that.'

Whoa! He knew they had a troublesome relationship, but he'd never realised that. Peter had shrugged off their clashes with the excuse that they were too alike. And he'd believed it.

'There's no need to look like that,' she reprimanded. 'It's not your fault.'

He wanted to make it better. Fix it.

He knew to his own detriment, though, that some things weren't fixable.

'How old were you when your mother left?'

'Eleven,' she replied.

'And she left your father for another man?'

'She did. And my father still hasn't got over it.'

Which was exactly why Will was never marrying. He was never opening his heart to that kind of damage.

Ahem, never marrying for real.

'Did she utterly abandon you and Peter?'

Sophie glanced down at her hands, and he found his own hands clenching to fists. 'Father made it difficult for her to see us.'

She should've tried harder!

'And seeing her tore him up every single time.' Her eyes grew shadowed. 'It was awful.' She lifted her chin and sent him a smile that made his heart ache. 'But it's ancient history. So tell me the deal with you and Lord Bramley.'

After her disclosure, it would be churlish to refuse to answer. He rolled his shoulders and tried not to scowl. 'From the age of fourteen he's tried to control every aspect of my life—where I went to school, what friends I had, all of my extra-curricular activities. I was never permitted to go camping with friends, or even on day trips with anyone he deemed unsuitable. And what was considered unsuitable was as changeable as the wind.' In the school holidays he'd basically been cut off from all of his peers. 'My only freedom was spending those few weeks in London with Peter. He liked Peter.'

For the first time since Peter's death, she smiled at the mention of his name. 'Everyone liked Peter.'

That was true.

'At least he chose good schools and good friends for you,' she offered.

He dragged both hands back through his hair, pulled air into suddenly cramped lungs. 'Look, I know I should be grateful to him for taking Carol Ann and me in when my parents died. And I am. But I'm now a grown man. I've earned the right to make my own decisions.'

She nodded. He could see her mind racing behind the perfect blue of her eyes and it occurred to him that she'd like to try and fix things for him the way he'd like to for her. It wasn't possible, unfortunately, and she'd come to see that in time too.

'Forcing me to marry is just the latest in a string of attempts to control my life. He sabotaged my university applications, which is why I spent my first year at St Andrews rather than the university in London I'd chosen. It took me a year before I could transfer.'

Her jaw dropped. 'That's… It's outrageous!'

He'd been furious at the time.

'That's messing with your whole…future! Your hopes and dreams and…and *everything*.'

Her outrage helped pour balm on the old wound.

He glanced at his watch.

'Yes, it's getting late,' she agreed.

Maybe he'd try and make their video conference earlier tomorrow. 'Is there anything else I should know?'

She shook her head.

'Before I forget, I had an account set up for you and the money transferred into it today. I'll email you the details.'

She swallowed and sent him a smile that wasn't really a smile. 'Thank you. I appreciate it.'

There was a mystery there. And he meant to get to the bottom of it.

Will tried to dam the shuffle of excitement that squirmed through him when he logged onto his laptop to dial in with Sophie the next evening—half an hour earlier than the previous evening.

She sent him a cheery wave from where she was nestled into one corner of the sofa, legs tucked beneath her. 'How was your day, dear?' she drawled in a Hollywood voice that made him laugh, even as it drew his skin tight.

'Busy. Filled with meetings. Yours?'

'Full of wedding prep.'

He grimaced, but she just shrugged. 'It hasn't been too bad, but your grandfather did give me a guest list of all the people he wanted to invite.'

Dear God. 'Did you agree to it?'

She rolled her eyes. 'Give me some credit, Will. I said I'd run it by you first. I'm trying to keep it small and contained—which I figured is what you'd prefer—but he's trying to blow it out into some kind of circus.'

He should be there fighting this battle with her.

She frowned. 'But maybe you'd prefer the circus.'

She couldn't be serious?

She took one look at his face and nodded. 'Right, scrap that. Just thought I'd check.'

'Who's on this guest list of his?'

'Well, we have two guest lists.'

Two?

'The apparently non-negotiable must-haves and the negotiable maybes.'

Great.

She stretched forward and just for a moment he thought he'd be gifted an unintentional eyeful of cleavage, but at the last minute she pressed her hand to the neckline of her blouse and all he was left with was an ache and the pounding in his veins. She settled back on the sofa with two sheets of paper and waved them at him. He grimaced. 'Hit me with the must-haves.'

She started reading them out. First came family—not that there was much of the Trent-Paterson line left. 'Okay.' He'd suck it up and endure them with as much grace as he could manage. 'That's not too bad.'

'Even counting Cousin Harold the potential usurper?'

He grinned at her mock ominous tones. He'd forgotten how playful she could be.

'Especially Harold. He'll be gnashing his teeth through the entire ceremony.' And he'd get his kicks where he could at the moment.

She laughed and that gave him a kick too.

'Next comes old family friends and neighbours,' she said, reciting the names.

He pursed his lips. 'We could cull half a dozen of those names, but...'

'What's the point?'

Exactly. 'Who's left?'

She wrinkled her nose. 'Dignitaries, local and otherwise.'

She rattled off the names and then a name came up that made him grimace. 'No way.'

She glanced up from the list.

'He's a local politician who's tried to model himself as some kind of philanthropist. Whenever he sees me—*every single time*—he tries to pump me for money...and then badgers me about improvements he believes are necessary to my grandfather's estate. It drives me crazy!'

She wrinkled her nose.

'And *every single time* he reminds me how I beat up his son when we were fourteen, implying that I owe him because he never called in the local authorities.'

She bit her lip, but her eyes danced. 'You beat up his son?'

He scowled and nodded.

'What did he do to deserve that?'

He didn't want to tell her. 'It sounds juvenile now,' he muttered.

She leant forward, more intrigued. 'You were fourteen. You're supposed to be juvenile.'

He pulled in a breath and then let it out in a rush. 'He used to sing my father's band's songs at me to wind me up. I ignored it for as long as I could. Eventually I told him to give it a rest or I'd beat him to a pulp. He kept going so...'

She covered her mouth with her hand and he

had a feeling she was holding back a wave of laughter. 'So you beat him to a pulp?'

'Not exactly. I just… I gave him a black eye.' And bloodied his nose.

She threw her head back and laughed. 'Good for you! Right, so we scrap them. There's only one more family on the list.'

She read the name out and he went cold all over. 'No.'

Her eyebrows rose, and he knew his face must look like thunder. All amusement vanished from her face. 'What did they do?'

It took a moment to unclench his jaw. 'I refuse to repeat the exact words, but they said the most disgusting things about Carol Ann and what should be done with her.'

Her eyes flashed and her every line grew so rigid the lists in her hands began to shake. She slashed a line through the names and called them such a rude word a laugh burst from him.

'I didn't know you had such a potty mouth,' he teased.

She stuck her nose in the air. 'I only pull it out on special occasions.'

He grinned. Good for her.

She turned her attention back to the list in her hand. 'Okay, so that means from your grandfather's list so far we have twenty-four names. You need to get me a list of who you'd like to invite.'

The short answer was nobody, but he knew that wouldn't wash.

'I've whittled my own list down to fourteen. The ten people my father would never forgive me for not inviting, and four of my closest girlfriends who'd be hurt beyond measure if I didn't include them. I thought we could keep it super simple and just have one attendant each. What do you think?'

Her words brought home the reality of what

they were doing. He'd never wanted to marry, but going through the motions of a sham wedding left a bad taste in his mouth.

The wedding isn't a sham.

The wedding would be legally binding.

Think of Carol Ann.

He pushed down a sigh. 'Who have you chosen?'

'Carol Ann.'

That made him smile. 'She'll be thrilled.'

'To bits,' she agreed.

If Peter were alive he'd have asked him to be his best man. But he wasn't. And in all honesty, he was far from certain that Peter would approve of this sham of a marriage. Especially given that Sophie was involved. But this arrangement was just as much to Sophie's benefit as to Will's. It would enable her to carve out the life for herself that she wanted. Surely Peter couldn't disapprove of that.

'Who is on my grandfather's other list—the wish list?' he asked, determined not to dwell on Peter in case Sophie guessed the direction of his thoughts.

She read them out. Half the names he didn't recognise, but luckily they came with additional descriptions like 'local publican' and 'chair of the golf club'.

'None of them,' he said. 'We're keeping this small.' Were they really going to go through with this?

'Excellent.' She crumpled the sheet into a ball and tossed it across the room.

He shook his head. Of course they were going to go through with it, but it didn't mean he had to enjoy it. 'Anything else I need to know?'

She shook her head.

'Then I'll sign off. Ring me if you need anything.'

CHAPTER FIVE

THE FOLLOWING NIGHT Will logged onto his main computer with its huge monitor. It would be more comfortable to use his laptop or tablet from the comfort of his living-room sofa, but he didn't want comfort. He wanted to keep this businesslike.

'How are things your end?' he asked when she came into view. And then gulped. He hadn't taken into account the effect of seeing Sophie on the big screen. He should've used his tablet after all. He made a mental note to use it the following night.

'Hello, Will, I'm fine. Thank you for asking. How are you?'

He closed his eyes and counted to three. 'I'm

glad you're fine. I'm well, thank you. Now, how did my grandfather react to the decimation of his guest list?'

'Threw a tantrum.'

He grimaced. 'I'm sorry. It's not fair that you have to put up with all of this.'

She shrugged, her gaze sliding away.

He stared at her and pursed his lips. 'Sophie, what did you do?'

She stuck out her chin and glared at him. 'I told him he'd interfered enough in your life as it was and that I wasn't letting him interfere any more. And that he better get used to it.'

She dusted off her hands and sent him a grin. 'Actually, it felt really good…which, perhaps, doesn't reflect all that well on me.'

He started to laugh. 'I'd have paid good money to see that.'

She rolled her eyes. 'You *are* paying good

money.' She bit her lip. 'Afterwards I did feel a bit mean, though. Like I'd kicked a puppy.'

'Do *not* allow that sulky, hard-done-by act to sway you. The man is a master manipulator.'

She winced. 'Well... I kinda fell for it, and kinda said he could have beat-up boy's dad on the guest list.'

She looked so contrite and hangdog he almost laughed.

'But I promise to run interference for you.'

He shook his head. 'I'm sure I'll survive.'

She sucked her bottom lip into her mouth and worried at it. Things inside him clenched up tight. 'Will, what's the worst thing he's done? Is the university thing his worst interference?'

A familiar anger—frighteningly cold—settled over him. 'Why?'

She lifted her arms and let them drop. 'I'm just trying to work out what else to expect.'

His every sense went on high alert.

'Your grandfather doesn't want you to marry me. He's going to do everything in his power to prevent it from happening. I've already corrected a few *mistakes* that have been made in relation to the dates with the caterers and the minister marrying us.'

And she was evidently up for the challenge. And while it was good to see her concentrating on something other than her grief, it didn't mean she needed to know his entire history.

He scratched both hands back through his hair. But there was a lot riding on this marriage. And knowledge was power. *Damn it!* He dragged in a breath and concentrated on his breathing rather than the icy rage pounding through him. 'You recall how distraught Carol Ann was when she came to live with me in London?'

She nodded.

'I found out later he'd filled her head with

all sorts of horror stories about the bad things that could happen to her in London. He made it sound like a hotbed of all things dire and disgusting—she was convinced it must be the most hostile place on earth.' *That* was the worst thing he'd done.

Her hand flew to her mouth. 'But...'

He just nodded.

She leaned forward, a frown filling her eyes. 'But that makes no sense. He adores her, dotes on her.'

'Anyone who'd deliberately frighten Carol Ann like that *cannot* really care for her.'

That frown deepened. 'He spends hours every day with her. I mean *hours*. They play board games, watch movies, go for walks. He truly dotes on her, Will. I think he was bluffing when he said she'd not have a home here at Ashbarrow.'

'I can't risk it. I don't trust him.' He couldn't

bear the thought of Carol Ann ever being that distressed again. 'Besides, you don't want to do yourself out of a million pounds, do you?'

'I don't want you forced into a marriage you don't want either.'

For some reason her words warmed him. 'While we're sharing private confidences… What's the worst thing your father ever did?'

She froze and he suddenly wished the question unsaid.

She eased away from the screen as if physically moving away from him. 'I promised to never tell.'

His gut started to churn. Dear God, had he hurt her physically? 'You promised your father?'

She shook her head. 'Peter,' she whispered. 'I promised Peter.'

He could tell from the expression in her eyes that it hadn't been a good promise to make.

'But it was all a long time ago now. It's ancient history. So stop looking so worried.'

She shot him a smile that pierced through the Teflon coating around his heart, and made his pulse pound.

'What we need to do is focus on the current problem—your grandfather.'

He bet it had something to do with her mother. He made a note to investigate the matter further—check the newspaper reports of the time.

She rolled onto her stomach and he suddenly realised that her laptop was perched on her bed. She was chatting to him from her bedroom. She was lying on her tummy...*on a big double bed.*

Erase that thought from your memory.

He swallowed. 'Do you have any thoughts?' She wore a tight vest top and it highlighted the gentle swell of her breasts, and it took all his concentration to keep his gaze on her face… though his peripheral vision refused to obey that command.

She wasn't wearing a scrap of make-up. Her hair was pulled up into some kind of messy bun. None of it should give her the appearance of a being a temptress. She wasn't trying to be a temptress, which only made it worse.

Tomorrow night he'd go back to talking to her on his tablet.

And then the night after that he'd be picking her up from the airport.

Hell!

'Will!'

He crashed back at the exasperation threading her voice. 'Sorry, I was miles away. Long day,' he lied.

It wasn't a lie. They were all long days.

'I was asking if there's something you could request or demand or be unequivocal about in relation to this wedding that would give your grandfather pause.'

'What kind of pause?'

'Something that would convince him you're really serious about this marriage.'

He had no idea.

'If you were ever to get married for real, what would you want? What's something personal, sincere…quirkily yours somehow?'

He stared at her. He didn't have a clue.

She stared back, the corners of her lips drooping. 'Well, you might want to give it some thought.'

He nodded.

She rested her chin in her hands. Her posture highlighted her cleavage, and thirst welled through him—incessant and demanding. He forced himself to keep his gaze on her face.

'A long day, huh?'

It was all he could do to nod.

'What do you do at that office of yours?'

'Meetings. I have a daily round of endless meetings.'

'With whom?'

'My different departments—Marketing and PR, HR, Legal, the development team. Then there are the clients. It used to be that I had to chase their business, but they approach me these days.' He could pick and choose the projects he worked on now. 'I'm in charge of project design. On top of that I've been brokering deals into previously closed markets overseas. All the usual stuff.

'What?' he demanded when she stared at him for a beat too long, feeling unaccountably defensive though he couldn't have said why.

'Do you enjoy it?'

The question made him blink. 'I like making money.' Money gave him freedom, independence, control. And he was never relinquishing those things. He was never allowing his life to be tossed around and disrupted on the whims of people like his parents or his grandfather—two extremes of the same pole. He was in charge of his own destiny now.

'Surely you've made enough of that by now.'

Had he?

'I remember you used to spend hours with the inner workings of a computer spread all around you, devising ways to make it run more efficiently and more powerfully. I used to marvel at your concentration. Do you still get to do that?'

Not any more.

Why not?

She cocked her head to one side. 'You know, the castle could do with an updated security system. I know it's not precisely your area, but it's all electronics, right?'

'You want me to design a security system for Ashbarrow?'

'Why not? You know the castle just about better than anyone. You'd know all of its security strengths—' her eyes danced '—and weaknesses.'

She grinned as if she'd known he'd developed ways of sneaking out of the castle and its grounds unnoticed as a teenager. He found himself grinning back. 'This is true.'

He sobered. 'Are you feeling unsafe at Ashbarrow?'

'Heavens no! Your grandfather employs a host of burly gardeners. But since the news of our engagement broke there's been a succession of reporters trying to get interviews. It's not a threat, just a nuisance.'

And one he could solve for her. She didn't need to put up with that. 'I'll get onto it straight away.'

* * *

'So the announcements in the newspapers weren't a joke? You're getting married?'

Sophie tried not to shrivel under her father's stunned glare. She forced her chin up, forced a smile to her lips, but she clung to Will's hand for dear life. 'Yes, at the end of the month. I spoke to your secretary and she's cleared your calendar.'

He drew himself up to his full imposing height of six feet four inches. 'Why so soon?' He glanced at her stomach.

'No, Father, I'm not pregnant. There's not going to be a surprise baby in six or seven months.'

'Then why this ungodly rush?'

He was as remote and unemotional as ever. The total opposite of Lord Bramley's thundering tantrums. 'Well,' she drawled. 'As I'm marrying Will for his money, I need to get him down the aisle as quickly as I can.'

She had the satisfaction of seeing a flash of fire whip through her father's eyes before they became studiously unemotional again.

'Sophie,' Will admonished, making her realise how childish she was being.

'I'm sorry, Will, you'll have to forgive my flippancy, but nothing I've ever done has met with my father's approval. Though I can't imagine how he can find fault with you.'

Her father's head rocked back. 'Of course I don't disapprove of William. He's a fine man. I just don't understand the urgency. Marriage is a serious undertaking…and people will talk at the ridiculous speed of your marriage.'

'And as we know, that's an argument that's always carried a lot of weight with me,' she drawled.

Will squeezed her hand. Oddly, it made her

feel less alone. The way Peter used to make her feel less alone.

'Why will you never be serious, Sophie?' Her father sighed.

Because she was tired of always being found wanting, though she didn't say that out loud. She didn't want him to know his disapproval could still wound her. 'All that was required of you was to offer your congratulations and wish us well.' She paused to give him time to respond. When he didn't she rushed on. 'The venue's booked and the invitations have gone out this morning. It's all prepared. I'm not changing the date now. Besides, people will talk more if the wedding is cancelled or delayed.'

His nostrils flared, his lips thinned, but if he'd wanted to reprimand her further he managed to hold himself back. 'And will I have the honour of walking you down the aisle?'

'I suppose people *will* talk if you don't.'

Could she be any more ungracious if she tried? She smothered a wince. Could he?

'Sir, I care for your daughter. I want the very best for her.'

'That's reassuring.'

'But there's something I've been wanting to ask Sophie, and it might be best if we all deal with that issue now…together.'

What on earth…?

'Sophie—' Will turned to her '—do you want your mother to attend the wedding?'

Her heart started to pound. Had he spoken to her mother?

As an eleven-year-old, she'd promised Peter to never speak of their mother to their father again. A rock settled in the pit of her stomach. She'd promised to never choose their mother over their father. *She'd promised.* But… Her pulse started to race and she couldn't look at her father.

She was an adult now. She no longer wanted to be anyone's pawn. Did she dare…?

She gazed into Will's eyes and it gave her the courage to face the fact that it was a promise she should never have been asked to make. It was a promise she didn't want to keep.

Not even for Peter.

She swallowed, her palms growing clammy. Her father had made it nearly impossible for their mother to keep in contact with them. It had been cruel and unfair. Still, looked at in the cold, hard light of day, her mother had relinquished all custody rights in exchange for an advantageous financial settlement.

She glanced at her father and wondered if he remembered that afternoon fifteen years ago. She moistened dry lips. 'If you want to walk me down the aisle, you need to speak to

Mother and tell her she's welcome to attend my wedding.'

The colour drained from her father's face. She gripped Will's hand and inched a fraction closer to him, her heart pounding like a caged thing. Will's hand tightened about hers. Without another word, her father turned and left the room.

A fist tightened about her ribcage until she could barely breathe. The last time she'd mentioned her mother to him…

'Sophie?'

She was dimly aware of Will pushing her into a chair and forcing her to take a sip of brandy.

She loved brandy, and it scorched a path down her throat now, burning off the shroud of mist that had her in its grip. Will crouched down in front of her, those dark eyes crinkling in concern as he scanned her face. 'Did I do the wrong thing in raising the topic of your mother?'

'No.' With an effort, she swallowed. 'You've spoken with her?'

He nodded. 'She cried when I told her why I was ringing.'

Really?

'She said nothing would give her more pleasure than to attend your wedding.'

So...she hadn't forgotten Sophie? Hadn't given up on her?

'She said she'd only be there, though, if she had both your and your father's blessings.'

Her throat thickened. She might not be eleven years old any more, but... 'I can't stay here tonight.'

He took one look at her face and didn't press her to explain or tell her she was being silly. 'You can come home with me unless you'd prefer a room at the Savoy.'

She'd prefer to be away from prying eyes. 'Your place will be perfect.'

'Wow!'

Sophie moved to the wall of glass in Will's converted warehouse apartment that overlooked the Thames. She'd been to his house in Chelsea, before he'd sold it—after Carol Ann's disastrous stay—but she'd never been here to his Canary Wharf penthouse.

The lights on the Thames glittered, turning the river into a fairyland. 'This is amazing.'

She turned with a smile. He'd been quiet ever since they'd left Knightsbridge and she wanted to lighten his mood. 'I definitely made the right choice. Your place has an even better view than a suite at the Savoy.'

He didn't so much as crack a smile. He took off his jacket and dropped it to the nearest chair. The broad lines of his shoulders made her pulse flutter up into her throat.

He moved across to stare down into her face. 'Sophie, has your father ever been violent towards you?'

His words momentarily froze her. Finally she managed to tip up her head to meet his gaze. She swallowed, the lie she'd started to form dissolving on her tongue. 'He's never slapped or hit me.'

'But?'

She swallowed again and nodded. 'He grabbed me once in anger. The look in his eyes, Will…' It had chilled her to the bone. For several long seconds her father's fury had made her fear for her life. She still had nightmares about it.

She chafed her arms. 'I had a puppy—a little terrier—and it flew to my defence and bit him on the ankle, which made him let me go.'

The puppy was gone the next day. She pulled in a breath. 'So he frightened me, but he didn't hurt me.'

And yet nothing had ever been the same again.

'Why did he grab you like that?'

She turned to stare out at the river, barely taking in the twinkling prettiness of it. 'I was being a brat. He was hauling me over the coals for my apparently disappointing school report...so I told him I missed my mother and wanted to see her. This was during their divorce. I knew it'd get a reaction out of him. I wanted to hurt him. I can't even remember now if I really wanted to see her or whether I just wanted to provoke him.'

'Sophie, you were eleven.'

And yet the memory was as vivid as if it had happened yesterday.

'You were frightened to stay in the house with him tonight.'

'Old ghosts,' she murmured. 'It reminded me of how ugly it all was when my mother first left. I didn't want to…revisit those memories.'

His eyes scanned her face and she prayed he'd let the matter drop. 'What memories, Sophie?'

A breath hissed out from between her teeth; she could probably deflect him, but she wasn't sure she wanted to. It felt strangely freeing to talk about it after all this time. She lifted her chin and met his gaze. 'That was the very last time I ever raised the topic of my mother in his presence, Will. Until this evening.'

His eyes widened, and his jaw slackened.

'You have to understand that my father really did terrify me that day. I'd never seen him so angry in all my life—not before and not since. My screams alerted the household staff…and Peter.'

The intensity of his gaze didn't waver. 'What happened afterwards?'

'I promised Peter I'd never mention my mother to Father again, that I'd never ask to see her or speak with her. I promised that if I had to appear in court I'd choose my father over my mother.'

Will stared at her, his face grey. He reached out and cupped her cheek. 'He should never have asked that of you.'

'No,' she whispered. 'I know he wanted to keep me safe, and that was part of it, but neither one of them should've asked that of me. I've been hiding from that fact all this time… until this evening.'

'When I put my foot in it.'

She pursed her lips, fear and exhilaration pounding through her in equal measure. 'It's time for me to take control of my life, Will. It's what I want to do. It's what I *need* to do. I want to get away from the party scene. And I no longer want to be a pawn in my father's on-going game of revenge. It's time that all ended.' It was time for her to be an adult.

Lord Bramley stared at her. 'Your mother is coming to the wedding?'

'We're hoping so.' She glanced at Will, who stared out of the drawing-room window, his back to them. He didn't turn around.

'But…does this mean your father is going to boycott the wedding?'

She couldn't work out if the idea appalled or appealed to him. 'I've no idea.' He'd refused to take her calls. She'd thought she wouldn't care a jot about that, but it appeared she did.

Will turned and his grandfather waved a finger at him. 'And you organised this? Didn't you know the hornets' nest you'd be stirring up? The Mitchell divorce case was…it was notorious at the time! And you want to go and rake all that up?'

'Don't start bellowing,' Will snapped. 'I knew what Sophie wanted and I set about making it happen. Lord Collingford will just have to deal with it. I won't have him bullying Sophie. If he wants to act like a child, then that's his affair.'

But his gaze darted to Sophie and she saw the uncertainty there. Before she could allay it, he'd rounded on his grandfather again.

'And while we're on the subject I won't have you bullying her either. You'll start by not challenging her every decision about this blasted wedding.'

'Blasted wedding?' Lord Bramley bounced onto the balls of his feet, stabbing a finger at the ceiling. 'Ha! I knew you didn't want this wedding!'

'I never wanted a wedding,' Will hollered back. 'If I'd had my way we'd have eloped to Vegas. It's only due to Sophie that we didn't. But in three Saturdays' time, Sophie gets the wedding she wants. And I'm not going to let anyone stop her from having it!'

Wow! He looked as if he meant every word.

He straightened. 'And, while we're on the subject of the wedding, I want Grandmother's wedding ring. I'd like Sophie to wear it.'

Double wow. For a moment the room went totally still. All the temper drained from Lord Bramley's face, though it was still grim—and behind the grimness lurked weariness. A part of her that she wanted to remain hard softened.

'You're both making the right noises, playing the roles of loving fiancés to perfection, but I'm not convinced the two of you haven't done some deal to try and trick me.'

'And what if we have?' she found herself saying. Both men swung to her, Lord Bramley's jaw dropping, Will's eyes throbbing though his face remained totally impassive.

'Yes, I know about your ultimatum. Of course Will told me about it. He's an honourable man. But because of your ultimatum you'll never know for sure now whether he marries for love or not. You seem to think you can just put some kind of schedule on love. Well, it doesn't work like that!'

She found herself pacing back and forth across the room, flinging her arms out as she spoke. 'And you know what—what's the big deal about love anyway? It didn't do my father any good. It didn't do Will's parents any good. Seems to me they'd have all been better off without it.'

The older man lowered himself into his armchair, brushing a hand across his eyes.

She wanted to yell at him that forcing Will into marriage was reprehensible, but she had a feeling he'd only hear the criticism implicit in the words, not the truth. For some reason he was hell-bent on bringing his grandson to heel. And nothing she said would change that.

She stopped pacing to slam her hands to her hips. 'Well, you know what? I think a marriage between two friends who like each other and respect each other has a better chance of success than either my parents' marriage or Will's parents' marriage, don't you?'

She stopped, breathing hard. Had she said too much? Had she ruined everything? She glanced across. Dear God, had she disappointed Will?

Will walked across, took her face in his hands and pressed a brief hard kiss to her lips that sent the blood stampeding through her veins. 'You're magnificent, you know that?'

She was?

'But it won't work,' he continued. 'You won't be able to guilt him into doing the decent thing. He won't let me off the hook.'

She bit back a smile. 'I don't really want you off the hook.' She had a million pounds to collect at the end of all this. Still, she wished he weren't in a position where he had no choice.

She glanced back at the older man, who stared at them with a frown in his eyes. 'I know you don't like me, Lord Bramley, but, whatever else you want to think, know this— I care about your grandson.'

She laced her fingers through Will's and it felt like the most natural thing in the world. 'You better get me out of here before I say something I really regret.'

A laugh rumbled from his throat. 'Your wish is my command.'

The older man shot to his feet. 'You'll be back for dinner?'

The expression on Will's face made her leap into the breach. 'Is Carol Ann expected home by then?' Will's sister was on an outing with a group of friends.

'Yes.'

'Then, yes,' she said over her shoulder as Will towed her from the room.

He didn't release her when they were out of their sight. If anything his grip tightened, and he scowled. 'I hate how he tries to control our every hour while we're here. Does he do that to you when I'm not here?'

'I'm rushed off my feet organising a wedding. He can't commandeer my time as and when he likes. He does like to know if I'm going to be in for dinner. But that's reasonable as he needs to let the cook know.'

Will stopped and stared down at her. 'Have you ever not been in for dinner?'

He asked as if the thought hadn't occurred to him. She nodded. 'I had a supper appointment with a prospective caterer last week.' It had been a blessing to get out from beneath Lord Bramley's oppressive surveillance.

She found herself grinning as she urged Will forward again. 'I took Carol Ann with me, which meant your grandfather had to dine alone. He sulked about it the entire day.' She hadn't felt the slightest bit guilty about it either. He'd been particularly tiresome that day, and she'd wanted to let him know she wouldn't put up with it.

'Where are we going?' she asked as he towed her towards the car.

'It's a surprise,' he said with a cryptic smile that immediately piqued her interest.

They drove for fifteen minutes before Will turned the car onto a country lane lined with tall hedges of hawthorn before turning into a driveway and pulling the car to a halt in a small car park. She read the sign and straightened. 'Moreland Park Equestrian Centre.'

She glanced through the windscreen, trying to take it all in. 'You've brought me to the local stables!'

'I thought you might like to have a look around. I phoned ahead so they're expecting us. The manager is going to give us a tour, which will give you an opportunity to ask all the questions you want.'

This was…perfect! She swung to him and he grinned at whatever he saw in her face. 'When did you arrange this?' Surely there'd been no time this morning?

'Through the week.'

His thoughtfulness touched her. 'Oh, Will, this is perfect. I can't thank you enough.'

He grinned and it made heat stir in her blood. Her fingers curled into her palms. She had to get these wayward feelings for Will under control. She had to stop thinking about him so… *carnally.*

'It's not entirely altruistic. I wanted to reinforce your reasons for being stuck out here in Scotland, help shore up any flagging defences.'

And just like that he made her laugh, and everything was comfortable again. Or, if not precisely comfortable, then at least contained. 'I always said you were a smart man.'

His gaze lingered on her lips for a couple of beats too long, but then he pushed out of the car. 'Ready?'

And she told herself she'd imagined the hunger that had momentarily flared in his eyes. She scrambled out of the other side. 'Yes, please.'

'So, what did you think?'

They were sitting across from each other in the quaintest of quaint tearooms—all frilly curtains, white tablecloths and perfect date scones—after their two-hour tour of the equestrian centre.

She lifted the teapot and poured them both cups of steaming tea, inhaling the fragrant brew as she blew on it. 'It was wonderful, brilliant. I mean, Morelands functions on a much larger scale than anything I'm planning, but...' She'd learned so much and her mind was reeling with it all. 'Have I thanked you yet?'

His smile hooked up one side of his mouth. 'Several times.'

'Good.' She took a sip of tea, before setting

her cup back to her saucer. 'It has me so eager to get started on my own place. I don't have the room to set up an eventing course like they have, but I could set up one of the fields with some small jumps.' And not so small jumps if she attracted clients who wanted them. 'Though I'd love to build an indoor arena like theirs.'

After Carla's treatment, hopefully there'd be enough money left to improve and update the current stables and outbuildings *and* stretch to an indoor arena as well. Apparently such facilities were in demand. And if she could attract expensive dressage horses to her establishment... Well, things could really take off!

Which might mean there wouldn't be enough money to stretch to a cottage initially, but she could have accommodation built into the stables. A flat with two bedrooms—one for her and one for Carla. Or maybe two flats. She'd need to look into prices, organise some quotes.

She suddenly became aware of how intently Will watched her and it made her skin prickle and her stomach tighten. Where earlier he'd watched her with a kind of pleased indulgence, now he'd turned almost grim.

She finished ladling strawberry jam onto a scone, but she didn't lift it to her lips. 'Did I totally screw up with your grandfather this morning?'

'No, you played it pitch perfect. It hadn't occurred to me to actually be honest with the old man. By mentioning the elephant in the room you...'

'I?'

'Deflated it. Robbed it of its power.'

She had? She could've sagged in relief. 'You know, if you hadn't told me about all the instances where he's interfered in your life, I'd have simply said he's all bluff and no bite.'

Except the expression in Will's eyes told her there was a lot of bite to the older man…and Will was just about fed up with it. And yet she couldn't dismiss from her mind how much time Lord Bramley spent with Carol Ann, how much he loved her.

'I think he's lonely.'

'I think he's scared that he's running out of people to lord it over,' Will countered.

'He hates London.'

Will's lips twisted. 'A fact he's made no secret of.'

She dragged her gaze from those lips. They had the ability to sidetrack her. And she didn't want to be sidetracked. She wanted to work Lord Bramley out. For Will's sake. After all, he was paying her a million pounds. She should do all she could to earn it. Working

Lord Bramley out was the least she could do. 'I mean, he *really* hates it. It's more than a rural man's disdain for the big smoke. It's…' She'd almost describe it as pathological.

She glanced at Will and bit her lip, wondering how he'd take any mention of his father.

He hadn't touched his tea. He hadn't touched his scone. And his grim gaze hadn't left her face. 'Go on.'

'Well, I wonder if he hates London so much because it's where your father died.'

He stilled before shifting in his seat. She couldn't decipher the expression on his face.

'Your parents' antics were well publicised.' Sex, drugs and rock 'n' roll seemed like the ultimate in bright-lights excitement, but from all she'd read it hadn't brought his parents much happiness. 'Maybe he blames London for the lifestyle choices they made.'

'No city can be blamed for my parents' bad behaviour.'

She winced at the hardness in his voice.

'My parents were hell-bent on self-destruction, and they didn't care how many people they hurt in the process or took down with them. It wouldn't have mattered if they were in London, Stockholm, Sydney or Pitlochry. Where they lived was the least of it.'

'But that's not exactly true, is it?'

His gaze speared to hers.

'There are more opportunities in a big city, more temptations. I mean, drugs are easier to get in London than they are in rural Perthshire.' Just look how easy it had been for Carla to fall under their spell.

'Don't be naïve, Sophie. Drugs are easy to get anywhere. With the right connections. And, believe me, my parents had the right connections.'

She prayed to God that Carla had no such connections in Surrey.

'Have you ever asked your grandfather why he's interfered so much?'

Will's jaw dropped. 'What for?' he demanded, snapping his jaw back into place. 'The man's a control freak. It's as simple as that. I'm not giving him the satisfaction of letting him list all of my so-called defects and character faults, or to reprimand me with all that I owe him.'

She lifted her cup and prayed her hand didn't shake. 'I think you should try talking to him.'

'Why?'

She set her cup down with a clatter. 'Because he took you and Carol Ann in when you were orphaned. Because he fed, clothed and housed you…sent you to good schools.'

His head rocked back as if she'd slapped him.

'Because it's still you who he wants to inherit the title and the estate.' Because she was certain that beneath it all, and despite appearances to the contrary, Lord Bramley loved his grandson.

'It's out of the question. And this subject is no longer open for discussion. What I do or don't owe my grandfather is no concern of yours.'

Ouch! So that told her.

He dragged a hand down his face. 'And it's not what I brought you here to discuss.'

So he did have something on his mind? But if it wasn't his grandfather and their current situation…? 'What did you want to discuss?'

'I had the money I sent to you tracked. I know it didn't go towards work at your stables. I want to know what you did with that money, Sophie.'

CHAPTER SIX

SOPHIE STARED AT Will in growing horror. 'You've…you've been *spying* on me?'

She found herself half out of her seat, but forced herself to sit back down. At the back of her mind a little voice kept whispering: *a million pounds, a million pounds*.

She couldn't create a scene. It wasn't just the money. She might be furious with him, but that didn't mean she wanted to wreck things for him where Carol Ann was concerned.

'I trusted you!'

He paled at her words, but his gaze didn't drop. 'I know the money was transferred to a medical facility in Surrey.'

She pushed all visible signs of anger deep

down until they couldn't be seen, making herself go completely blank. She'd had plenty of practice doing that with her father.

'It appears you've just answered your own question, then,' she said, reaching for her scone, forgoing the cream. She wasn't sure she could face a scone with just jam as it was. 'So I wonder at you bothering to ask the question at all.'

His eyes narrowed. 'Sophie, I—'

'What is it with you and your grandfather? Is it a genetic thing that makes you want to control everyone in your vicinity?'

He leaned towards her, eyes flashing. 'I am *nothing* like my grandfather.'

His voice was tight and hard, and she forced herself to give a tinkling laugh designed to set his teeth on edge. His jaw clenched and she tried to feel a measure of satisfaction. 'Darling, from where I'm sitting you could be one and the same person.'

She bit into her scone and watched his hands clench and unclench on the table.

'Why did you send a hundred thousand pounds to this medical facility?'

'A donation.'

'I don't believe you.'

'I don't care,' she flashed right back.

Damn! She was supposed to be channelling a glacial composure, not lashing out in anger… and hurt. 'I told you that you had no say in how I spent the money. I'm wondering what else you're now going to renege on. What else are you going to demand for your million pounds, Will?'

His mouth went tight. 'I want to know what kind of trouble you're in!'

'I'm in no trouble whatsoever.'

'I want to believe you.'

Her heart pounded so hard her chest started to ache. 'But you don't?' She shook her head, searching for that comforting blankness, finding herself absurdly close to tears. 'I suppose I shouldn't find that so surprising. Or disappointing.'

He swore, low and savage, and she dropped her scone to her plate and reached for a napkin. She pressed it to her lips, her stomach churning.

'There's too much at stake here, and I'm not talking about the money. I don't care about the money. Hell, Sophie, you think I enjoy asking you this? I'm caught between a rock and a hard place, and I'm going to be flattened whichever option I choose. Maybe you can provide me with some advice for this particular dilemma.'

She had no idea what he was talking about.

'Do I trust you and hope for the best? Or do I keep faith with the promise I made Peter?'

Her heart burned at the mention of her brother's name. She moistened suddenly dry lips. 'What did you promise Peter?'

He sat back, dragged a hand through his hair. 'To look out for you. To help you if you were ever in trouble. To be there for you when he couldn't.'

Her brother had died in Africa. He'd been a pilot for a charity organisation in charge of establishing hospitals in remote areas. He'd flown in building supplies and provisions. However, hostile rebel forces had surrounded one of the villages he'd flown into and there'd been no chance of escape. During the six-hour stand-off, he'd rung to tell her he loved her. The memory of that phone call made her temples throb. The authorities hadn't arrived in time to save them. The entire village had been slaughtered.

'When did you make that promise?'

'The day he died. He called you first and then your father…and then me.'

She hadn't known he'd called Will too. The two of them had never spoken about it.

Just for a moment her mother's face swam into vision and she had to close her eyes against a different pain. 'Would you keep a promise made to Peter, even if it were a bad promise?'

'Sophie, it was the last thing I ever promised him.' Pain made his voice hoarse. 'Don't ask me to break my word to him.'

For a moment she had to cover her face with her hands.

'Please…won't you confide in me?'

She heard the agony stretching behind those words and it dissolved her anger. He was trying to do his best by Peter. She couldn't blame him for that.

She lifted her head. 'To confide in you means

I have to break a promise I've made to someone else.'

'Peter?'

Not Peter. To someone who hadn't been
thinking clearly…who still wasn't thinking
clearly. An unexpected surge of relief at the
thought of sharing her burden momentarily
blindsided her. But…

She lifted her chin. 'I'll make a deal with
you, Will.' Not that she was in a position to
make a deal, but… If something good could
come from breaking her promise to Carla,
she'd take it.

'What kind of deal?'

'I'll confide in you…'

'And in return…?'

'You speak to your grandfather—really talk
to him. Try and find out why he's so insistent
you marry, try and find out why he's interfered
so much in your life.'

He didn't draw back as she expected. He gave a hard nod. 'Deal.'

Wow. She swallowed and glanced around the cosy tearoom. 'I can't break a promise in such civilised surroundings. Can we go somewhere…wild?'

Without a word he rose, tossed some money on their table and led her out to the car. Ten minutes later she found herself halfway up a mountain with a green windswept valley spread out below. Lochs glinted in the intermittent sun as low clouds scudded across the sky, and when she pushed out of the car the wind whipped her hair about her face.

'Is this wild enough?'

'It's perfect.' Pulling a hair tie from her pocket, she drew her hair back into a ponytail. She planted herself on a boulder and stared at the view. Will stood beside her, although there was room enough for him to sit on the rock too. He stuck his hands into his pockets and braced his legs against the wind and just waited. He didn't prompt or pressure her and she was grateful for it. In fact, she found his presence somehow reassuring.

Finally she moistened her lips and started to speak. 'I sent the money to that medical facility in Surrey because Carla is currently in drug rehab there. It's the first instalment of money for treatment that we expect will cost three hundred thousand pounds. I paid twenty thousand pounds a month ago to hold her place, but that pretty much cleaned me out.'

She'd been too busy trying to escape from the harsh reality of Peter's death and hiding from her grief to save money. It made her sick to the stomach with shame now. How could she have been so frivolous? How could she have been so blind?'

From the corner of her eye she saw Will turn

towards her, sensed he was about to speak. She held up a hand. 'Please don't say anything yet. Let me just…finish.' She swallowed. She couldn't look at him. 'And don't look at me— look at the view. I'm betraying Carla's confidence in telling you this, and I've let her down so much already that I don't think I can stand for you to watch while I…'

She couldn't finish the sentence. Will turned to stare back at the view. She wanted it to help. She wanted it to ease the burning in her chest, help her breathe more freely, but it didn't. She forced herself to continue. 'I needed to pay a significant proportion of the money by the end of this week. They were threatening to stop her treatment unless monies were received.'

She could hardly blame them. They deserved payment for all their hard work. They were providing Carla with the very best care.

She glanced down at her hands. 'I know there

are cheaper treatment options available, but this particular programme has had outstanding results and came highly recommended. I want Carla to have the very best treatment available.' She wanted Carla to have every chance for a bright and happy future.

She sensed rather than saw Will nod.

'You see, I wasn't even aware that Carla was doing drugs. I was too wrapped up in my own little world—too busy dancing into the wee small hours, guzzling champagne, going home with whoever took my eye…all while trying to forget that Peter was no longer with us. I didn't know Carla had taken it to a whole other level with drugs—snorting cocaine at every available opportunity, apparently. Not until one of my old school friends told me about the rumours she'd been hearing.'

That conversation had been the first slap back to reality.

The second had been finding Carla with a needle in her arm.

'By the time I cottoned on to what was happening, Carla had moved to heroin.' A better friend would've noticed sooner.

Will swung back to her. 'Can I speak yet?'

His voice shook with emotion, and it was all she could do not to throw herself into his arms and sob her heart out. She blinked hard and nodded.

'How did you convince her to get treatment?'

That hadn't been easy. 'She flat out refused at first. We had the most dreadful row.' She stared at a cow grazing far below them and refused to take her eyes from it. 'It was awful. I think it shocked her into realisation—that she was killing herself, that she was in danger of losing everything, that she needed help… that the path she was on was not the one Peter would've wanted for her.'

'Do her parents know?'

She shook her head. 'She made me promise not to involve them. She made me promise not to tell anyone.' A promise she'd now broken. 'I'm not permitted to see her at the moment—it's part of her treatment.' She pulled in a deep breath. 'It's also part of her treatment to tell those closest to her about her condition. She doesn't know that yet.'

She had no idea how Carla would cope with it. She just prayed her friend would find the courage and the resources she needed when the time came. 'Before I laid down any cold hard cash I had a long talk with one of the doctors in charge of the programme.' He'd explained the process to her. 'There're no easy fixes. She has a long road ahead of her.'

She moved her eyes from the grazing cow to stare at the way the light played across the surface of a loch, making it look blue one moment and silver the next. There was hope for Carla. That bright future was still there waiting for her to claim it. But she should never have fallen so far before Sophie had noticed.

Will crouched down in front of her, blocking out the loch and the cow and forcing her to meet his gaze. She expected to see censure—she deserved censure—but there was only concern…and warmth. Her throat thickened.

'Soph, have you been dealing with this all on your own?'

The affectionate shortening of her name made her eyes fill. She swallowed, hard. 'It was the least I could do.'

'And that's the reason you wanted a million pounds—for Carla's treatment.'

She blew out a breath. 'I really only needed three hundred thousand.'

'But?'

She bit back a sigh and tried to find a smile. 'But I want a place where Carla can come to once her treatment is finished. And, at the risk of sounding like your grandfather, I wanted that to be away from London with all its temptations and associations. She deserves a chance at a fresh start.'

'And, like you, she's a rider,' he said slowly.

She should've twigged that something was wrong when Carla had stopped riding with her.

'I'd have given you the money, no strings attached, if you'd told me.'

She knew that. 'I made her a promise. I wanted to keep it.'

'But I forced you to break it.'

She shrugged, surprised to discover she didn't feel guilty. Not about that, anyway. 'You invoked Peter's name.' It still had the power to trump everything else. 'And I knew that if I didn't tell you, you'd investigate further and discover the truth for yourself. Besides…' She hesitated.

'What?'

'I'm glad someone else knows. I'm glad someone else has her back if she needs it.'

Will stared into blue eyes cloudy with concern and remorse and had to fight the urge to haul her into his arms and hold her close. He had a feeling that offering Sophie physical comfort could lead all too easily to other things.

And he'd promised her no complications.

Her life evidently had enough of those already. It made him wonder if he'd ever truly known her.

A headache started up behind the backs of his eyes. He'd forced her to betray a confidence. It had been a despicable thing to do, and yet… 'I wish I'd known about this sooner. I'd have helped.'

He understood why she hadn't, of course. She'd handled everything extremely well from what he could tell. But it tore at him that she'd had to deal with it alone. He rose and took a step back before the sweet plum-jam scent of her addled his brain.

She shot to her feet and made as if to seize his arm, but obviously thought the better of it and let her hand drop to her side. 'Would you have done it differently?'

'No!' He didn't want her thinking that. 'I could've just been a support for you.'

'For me? I don't deserve anyone's support! I let Carla down. If it wasn't for me she wouldn't be in this mess at all.'

He stiffened. 'That's nonsense! You didn't buy her the drugs. You didn't urge her to take them.'

'Maybe not, but before Peter she hardly ever went out to nightclubs or wild parties. She'd have never run with a fast crowd if it weren't for me. That was my doing. She became my partying partner in crime.'

He could see now, so clearly, how both women had been trying to hide from their grief.

'I should've taken better care of her. I should've realised sooner what she was up to.'

'People with drug problems learn to hide it.' He hauled in a breath. 'People have to make their own choices. And holding yourself responsible for Carla's drug addiction won't help you get over your grief for Peter any more than partying for two years has.'

She flinched, and he wanted to swear. He reached out and grasped her shoulders. 'Why can't you focus on the positives? Why can't you acknowledge the good you're doing now?'

'The good?' She jerked out of his grip. 'What on earth can be positive about any of it?'

'That Carla *is* getting the help she needs,

that you've been instrumental in getting her that help.'

'But—'

'No buts, Sophie.'

She stared at him, confusion and consternation chasing themselves across her face.

'I want you to know something else.'

She gripped her hands in front of her as if waiting for some kind of judgement or condemnation. A part of him started to weep for her. 'I want you to know that I do trust you. I'm sorry I asked you to break your word to Carla. I should've known better. I won't make that same mistake again.'

Her eyes widened.

'I made a promise to Peter, which means I'll still ask questions if I'm concerned about anything, but if you tell me to back off and mind my own business, I will.'

'I...' She snapped her mouth closed, evidently at a loss for what to say. She didn't have to say anything.

'You're not a child who needs checking up on, but a woman who knows her own mind—an adult who can look after herself and the people she cares about. My loyalty lies with the living.' He dragged in a breath and made himself continue. 'My loyalty lies with you now, rather than Peter.' And in his bones he felt that this was exactly what Peter would've wanted.

Will settled in front of his giant computer monitor half an hour earlier than his and Sophie's scheduled meeting time. For the last two evenings, though, she'd been ready a good twenty minutes early.

But as he sat there waiting, he realised she wasn't going to be early tonight.

He frowned. Had she mentioned that she had some meeting scheduled for the evening?

A moment later he shook his head. It could simply be his grandfather commandeering as much of her time as she'd allow. While Sophie had won points for her forthrightness last Saturday, his grandfather had still monitored her every movement on Sunday…and that same suspicion continued to lurk in his eyes, even if it had become tempered with a dash of uncertainty.

He found himself scowling. Why didn't she just make some excuse and pop to her room to see if he was here yet or not?

He knew he wasn't being fair. She knew he'd had an important dinner and drinks meeting this evening. She couldn't know he'd left early. She couldn't know that chatting to her every night had become the highlight of his day.

He rolled his shoulders, stretched his neck first one way then the other. Frowned. It wasn't so much a *highlight* as a relief that their charade had survived another day, and that she was still coping with being stuck in Ashbarrow.

He pulled a notepad towards him and spent the next thirty minutes sketching out ideas for a new security system for the castle.

He spent the following ten minutes drumming his fingers and wondering why Sophie was late.

Thirteen and a half minutes later, Sophie logged on. She smiled and waved when she saw him. She always started their meetings with a wave. It was kind of cute.

'You're home! I wasn't sure you'd make it back in time for a meeting tonight.'

He shrugged, trying to look nonchalant as every cell fired to life at the sight of her. She was lying on her back. Her laptop must be balanced on her stomach…or higher. Perspiration prickled his nape. 'We finished early.'

'Nice.'

'While you've been running overtime,' he couldn't resist pointing out. Common sense told him to drop it. It was only a few minutes. 'How's your day been?'

Her eyes narrowed as if she'd sensed his mood, but she didn't pursue it. 'Wedding prep is progressing nicely.'

'Have you rung your mother yet?' He'd given her the number.

She sat up and crossed her legs, placing the computer and him at a further distance. 'Have you talked with your grandfather yet?'

Touché. It was all he could do not to let loose with a rude word.

'Also, I spoke too soon when I said your grandfather had dispensed with his fun and games. He's back to his old tricks.'

He fought the urge to drop his head to his

arms. He had to hand it to the old man—he had staying power. 'What's he done now?'

'We have a new house guest.' She rolled her eyes. 'Christian Dubois.'

His jaw dropped. How the hell did his grand-father know the world's most in-demand male model?

'Apparently Christian's grandfather and Lord Bramley were at college together,' she said, as if she'd seen the question in his face. 'Christian has been in the Highlands shooting some af-tershave advertisement. You know the kind— all manly trout streams and drinking whisky in front of a roaring fire.'

In a recent poll, Christian had been voted one of the world's most beautiful men. The pencil Will held snapped. 'Is he as good-looking in the flesh as they claim?'

'Physically the man is an absolute god.'

Pencil lead powdered his fingers. He stared

at the fistful of crumbling shards and tossed them into the waste-paper basket beneath his desk.

'Unfortunately,' Sophie continued, 'the illusion is shattered the moment he opens his mouth.'

Her subtle assurance should've reassured him, but something ugly had started to press against his breastbone. He did his best to dispel it. 'Full of himself?'

She shook her head. 'It's not so much that. I...' She hesitated before stretching out on her front and moving closer to whisper, 'Dear God, Will, the man is so vain! He keeps trying to catch glimpses of himself in any available reflective surface—mirrors, windows... the silver teapot. He acts as if there's a camera trained on him at all times. Unfortunately, he also likes the sound of his own voice.'

Her grimace almost made him laugh.

'What *is* amusing, however, is that as your grandfather is the one who invited him here he's the one who has to entertain Christian and sit there and listen to him boast about his exploits.'

That picture did make him laugh. A moment later he sobered. 'I take it you think he's invited Christian in the hopes the two of you will…hit it off.'

'Seems the likeliest explanation, don't you think?' She shrugged. 'Though, who knows? I'm starting to think your grandfather could make the sanest person paranoid.'

Spots flashed in front of his eyes at the thought of Sophie with Christian. 'Are you tempted?' he found himself growling. Had she and Christian been…*getting to know each other better*? Was that why she'd been late?

Her eyes widened, and then they flashed

with an unfamiliar fire. 'I seem to recall that I promised you discretion.'

He folded his arms and leaned back. 'Are you *discreetly* tempted? If any of this makes the papers...'

That damn chin came up and her eyes grew as hard as his must be. 'It's two weeks to our wedding. I'm in your grandfather's house. I'm not sure what your definition of discreet is, but I can assure you that's not mine.'

He couldn't stop himself. 'And yet I notice you haven't actually answered the question.'

'I've no intention of dignifying such a ridiculous question with an answer either!'

He was being an idiot. But the strength of the protest running through him had taken him completely off guard. He owed her an apology, but he couldn't force the words from his throat.

His hands balled to fists. 'I want you to stay away from Christian Dubois.'

'That's becoming increasingly evident,' she shot back, colour high on her cheeks. 'You took such pains to let me know how much you trusted me on Saturday, but words are cheap, Will. I've no intention of cuckolding you before the wedding. You know I've no intention of making you look a fool. And, I've told you, I can't bear the man!'

It was true. He knew that in his head. But at the moment he was operating with a different part of his anatomy. Not even his anatomy but some strange beast that lurked inside him.

'So what are you really scared of?'

'I'm not scared of anything,' he shot back, stung.

'Then why are you shouting?'

Both of their voices had risen, and then he heard Sophie's bedroom door bang against the wall as if it had been flung open. Christian? He actually growled.

Sophie's head rocked back to stare at a point beyond him and then he heard his grandfather shouting. 'I heard voices! I knew you had someone in here. I...'

The expression on Sophie's face made Will wince.

She swung her laptop around and the room swam and dipped, making his stomach reel with vertigo. And then his grandfather came into view.

Will didn't uncross his arms. He didn't say hello. His grandfather's gaze met his and the older man visibly swallowed.

'I thought...' The old man trailed off, looking suddenly old.

'Get out of my room.'

Sophie's voice shook with so much suppressed emotion Will wanted to punch something.

'My dear—' his grandfather's mouth worked '—I'm sorry. I—'

'Now!'

She shouted the word so loud it all but deafened him. Without another word the older man turned and hastened from the room. Sophie appeared in his monitor again and he found himself swallowing at the anger livid in her face. 'I don't like either one of you at the moment.'

She couldn't put him in the same category as his grandfather!

'Don't even think about coming up here.'

How did she know he was?

'Because I'm in absolutely no mood to see you.'

'But—'

And then she snapped the lid of her laptop closed and everything went dark. She hadn't even said goodnight! He swore and swore… and swore some more.

He tried her phone, but his call went to voice-mail. He sent her an email. She didn't reply. He checked flights to Inverness, but it was too late to fly out tonight. What the hell was he thinking? He couldn't fly to Scotland now. He paced the wall of windows that overlooked the Thames. He had important meetings in the morning. He couldn't fly out tomorrow either.

He pulled in a deep breath. And then another. He'd call Sophie tomorrow, once she'd calmed down. He'd give her a chance to cool off to-night, and then he'd apologise so abjectly she'd have no choice but to forgive him.

Tomorrow.

And tomorrow he might look into who among his staff could adequately represent him at all of these blasted meetings. Sophie was right—he had more money than he knew what to do with. He should be enjoying life, not wasting it on some corporate treadmill.

Sophie refused to pick up Will's calls the next day, so he finally ventured to ring the house itself. The housekeeper passed the phone to his grandfather rather than Sophie. It took all his strength not to hang up, but any news of Sophie would be better than none at all.

'Will, my boy,' his grandfather started in a hearty tone that immediately set Will's teeth on edge.

'I don't want to talk to you. Put Sophie on.'

'She, uh… She's not here.'

Not there? 'Where is she?' He roared the words. He couldn't help it.

'I don't know!' his grandfather roared back. 'She left a message with the housekeeper that she'd be out all day. And she's not answering her phone.' There was a short pause. 'I understand why she's not taking my calls, but why isn't she taking yours?'

'Because I made an absolute cake of myself last night because of Christian—thanks for that, by the way. I acted like a jealous idiot!' He raked a hand through his hair. He hoped to God she'd not washed her hands of the lot of them.

'I'm sorry.'

He blinked. Had his grandfather just…apologised?

'Christian has gone, if that helps at all. I… I've evidently misjudged the lass.'

'You have.' But then so had he.

'I—'

His grandfather broke off. Will heard voices in the background, and then Carol Ann's excited voice burbled down the phone. 'Will, I got a new dress.'

He did what he could to inject enthusiasm into his voice. 'What colour?'

She laughed. 'Purple, of course, silly! It's for the wedding.'

He swallowed. 'You'll be the prettiest girl there.'

'Second prettiest. Sophie will be the prettiest. And I have *another* new dress too.'

'Two new dresses?'

She chortled at his mock shock. 'For Sophie's dad's party on Saturday.'

He straightened. 'You're coming to the ball?' Carol Ann was coming to London? *And* she was excited about it? His heart started to pound.

'Sophie invited me. She said there'd be cake and dancing.'

Sophie had…

'And she said that when you're married I can come visit in London and that…and that you'll take me to musicals!'

His throat thickened. 'That sounds like fun.'

'And we can have afternoon tea at the Ritz, and walks in the park to feed the squirrels, and…and I can't remember all the things Sophie said we could do, but they were all fun! And I want to do them all. I can, can't I?'

'Sure you can. I can't wait!'

'Good, 'cause Sophie said I could stay in your big apartment when I come to London—that I can have my very own room there.'

He couldn't speak for the lump that lodged in his throat. Sophie had… All this time she'd been quietening Carol Ann's fears about London? And he'd repaid that by—

He choked back an oath. He slumped against the wall, sliding down until he sat on the carpet.

'But on Saturday night I'm having a slumber party in her room at her dad's house.'

'I want to have a slumber party with you and Sophie on Saturday night too.'

Carol Ann laughed as if that was the funniest thing she'd ever heard. 'You can't, silly! And you know what else, Will?'

'What?'

'She's going to teach me to ride too.'

He blinked. Horses had always intimidated Carol Ann.

'When I go stay with her in Cornwall she said I could choose my own pony just for me. And she said we could be best friends forever.'

His head spun. 'Who? You and Sophie or you and the pony?'

'The pony, silly! Me and Sophie are already BFFs.'

And Sophie had used that influence to turn Carol Ann's unreasonable fear of London on its head. She'd given his sister something tangible to love about London—things to look forward to. Her kindness and generosity blew his mind.

Acid burned his stomach at his behaviour the previous evening. 'I can't wait to see you in your purple dress, Carol Ann. Can you give Sophie a message for me when she gets back?'

'Uh huh.'

He had a vision of his little sister nodding earnestly.

'Can you tell her that I wish that I could kiss her?'

Carol Ann giggled but promised to pass the message along.

'I love you, Carol Ann.'

'I love you, Will.'

CHAPTER SEVEN

BLAST! THERE WASN'T a darn thing left to do—nothing left to fuss and tinker with, nothing left to turn her attention to.

Sophie prowled through the ballroom of one of London's premier hotels casting a critical eye over the round tables covered in crisp linen, set with sparkling crystal and gleaming cutlery, and topped with pink-and-cream peony centrepieces, which even she had to admit were rather fabulous. Pity the perfection couldn't ease the burning in her soul.

She glanced at the pink and gold balloon displays that marched down the length of the room between French doors that led out to the paved terrace and wondered what it would be like to feel that light and buoyant. She felt as if someone had dropped a stone weight on her shoulders.

Stop being a drama queen. Stop overreacting.

But no matter how often she told herself that, it did nothing to lessen the weight pressing down on her. If only she could work through this tangle of emotions and—

She slammed to a halt, her thoughts scattering when a familiar figure appeared at the far end of the ballroom.

Will.

She swallowed. For the last three days she'd refused to take his calls or to return them. She'd refused to answer his emails. She'd been strung tight at the thought of seeing him tonight, so it made no sense to feel suddenly… lighter.

She inclined her head towards the one set of French doors that were open. He reached them before she did and stood aside to let her pass first. She did her best not to breathe in the dark, spiced lime scent of him too greedily.

Wordlessly, she selected a bench in the sun. He chose the one opposite in the shade. Crossing her legs, she met his gaze. She saw what she expected to see—what his phone and email messages had been full of—worry, regret, contrition. She hadn't thought seeing those things would help. But somehow it did.

She saw too what she hadn't expected to see—anger…and resentment? Or was it frustration?

Whatever it was, it made her heart pound.

He leaned towards her. 'Are you okay? I've been worried sick!'

'I'm fine.'

'That's not what my grandfather has been saying.'

She raised an eyebrow. 'You've been speaking to your grandfather?'

He threw himself backwards and scowled at her. 'I had to speak to someone. You wouldn't!'

She shrugged. 'I didn't feel like talking to you.'

'You made that clear.'

He leapt to his feet and paced up and down in front of her, hands clenching and unclenching, spine stiff. She considered patting the bench beside her and then thought the better of it. It might be wise to keep all of that unchecked energy at one remove.

'I was offended—*really* offended—at what you implied when we last spoke.'

He stopped pacing to stare at her with hooded eyes. 'I acted like a jerk. Sophie, I'm sorry. I've wanted to apologise ever since it happened.'

'I know. I've listened to your messages… read your emails.'

'But you wanted me to stew?'

She shrugged. 'You don't get to act like a jerk

and expect no consequences, Will. Not even for a million pounds.'

His jaw dropped.

'And I needed time to think.'

He sat back on the bench opposite, his face shaded by a tulip tree. 'My grandfather and I have treated you abominably. I wouldn't blame you if you wanted to pull the pin on the wedding.'

She'd love to. But she couldn't. 'I'm not going to do that,' she started slowly. 'But I do have some concerns.'

His gaze sharpened. 'Tell me.'

He wanted to fix it, make things right. It almost made her smile. But then her concerns pressed down on her again and any desire to smile fled. 'Why were you so jealous, Will? I mean, despite the fact it was a needless jealousy…why did you lose the plot so completely?'

He shook his head. 'Because I'm an idiot.'

'Not good enough,' she said softly.

His gaze speared to hers.

'You've said in all your messages that you trust me, that you know I'd not do anything to jeopardise our…arrangement.'

'I meant all of that.'

'But the thing is…you were jealous.' She moistened dry lips. 'Which would indicate that you've developed feelings for me.' And that frightened her out of her wits. Every atom of her being screamed that she needed Will in her life. Sex would ruin that.

And love was out of the question.

Will's head rocked back. 'I don't *do* the kind of feelings you're hinting at, Sophie.' He shot to his feet, raking both hands back through his hair. 'I mean, I have feelings for you. Of course I do. Our lives are entwined. You mean a lot to me. But I *don't* have romantic feelings for you.'

She let out a breath and waited for relief to wash over her. And kept waiting.

'It's true that my feelings have recently become more—' he swallowed '—carnal.'

Her every cell snapped to attention before her muscles grew languorous with need. *Oh, no, no!* They couldn't go there. They'd already spoken about it!

'But I promised our relationship wouldn't turn physical. And I mean to keep my word.'

He stared at her, his lips set, his eyes proud and angry, and Sophie suddenly realised where that resentment and frustration she'd sensed earlier originated. There was an answering surge of those same things firing through her blood now. She couldn't answer him. She could only nod.

'It'll pass,' he growled.

Good to know. She nodded again.

He jammed his hands into his pockets. 'I

panicked on Wednesday night because the stakes of this game are so high. And so many of the variables are outside of my control. I...' He hesitated. 'I hate that I have to rely on you to help me secure Carol Ann's future.'

That might just be the most honest thing he'd ever said to her.

'I hate that you're stuck in the Highlands when that wasn't part of the original deal.'

She shrugged. 'That's no biggie.'

'I hate that you've had to put up with my grandfather's nonsense.'

The older man had overstepped the mark on Wednesday night, and he knew it. In his own way he was as contrite as Will. He'd been carefully polite and solicitous ever since. 'I think that's all going to change now.'

'You shouldn't have had to deal with any of it in the first place.'

'When are you going to talk to him?'

He glanced away and she smothered a sigh. But she understood. 'I spoke to my mother last night.'

He swung back. 'How did that go?'

She wasn't really sure. 'She said she'd love to come to the wedding, but she'd only be there if my father assured her she was welcome.'

Apparently her daughter's blessing wasn't enough.

Will's hands clenched to fists. 'And your father…?'

She shrugged, though it took an effort to maintain a semblance of nonchalance. 'I told him this morning what I expected of him. Now I just need to wait and see if he delivers.' Or not.

'And you're…?'

'Passing Adulting for Beginners with flying colours,' she said. He stared at her with unconvinced eyes and she folded her arms. 'I'm fine, Will. You've no need to worry about me.'

He tapped a fist against his chin. But finally straightened and nodded. 'There are a lot of things I hate about our current situation, but I can't tell you how much I appreciate all you've done for Carol Ann. Is she really coming to the ball tonight?'

'She and Esther are at my father's place as we speak.'

'I don't know how you managed to contrive such a miracle, but I can't thank you enough.'

That had been easy. She'd simply started peppering their conversations with all the fun things Carol Ann could do in London if she ever came to visit. The fact that Sophie loved London so much had inevitably rubbed off too.

She'd raved about *The Sound of Music* and *Mamma Mia!* theatre adaptations she'd seen, had described in exquisite detail what a high tea at the Ritz looked like. She'd just filtered a little bit of London into the conversation here and there every day, managing to pique Carol Ann's curiosity, interest…and eventual eagerness to sample such delights for herself. 'She deserves to not be afraid.'

She forced herself to her feet. 'Will, I don't actually want you to be forced into a marriage you don't want. If you decide to rethink this whole scheme, I'd certainly understand. I wanted there to be other options if things… fell through.'

She couldn't read the throbbing in his eyes as they stared into hers. 'You have to understand that wanting to visit London and wanting to live here are two very different things. I don't know if Carol Ann could ever adapt to that.'

'True, but a start has been made.' With time, and a lot of patience, Will could help Carol Ann make that transition.

'Our marriage is still the best way to secure my sister's future.'

She swiped her hands down her skirt and nodded again, tried to force a businesslike crispness to her voice. 'Right, we'll call that Plan A, then. You still need to speak to your grandfather before the wedding, and you still have to get him to sign your legal papers.'

He set his jaw. 'Next weekend.'

'Excellent. Now, are you still sure you want to attend tonight's ball? Everyone is talking about our engagement. There'll be questions and comments, some good-natured teasing—' who knew? maybe some not-so-good-natured teasing as well '—and the press.'

His lip curled. 'You make it sound so enticing.'

She was just giving him the unvarnished truth. 'I know how much you hate any kind of publicity or attention. On the plus side, however, there'll be a beautiful meal, and dancing with me and Carol Ann later.'

'What man could resist that?'

The smile didn't reach his eyes, and she found she couldn't smile either.

'You don't think I can handle this evening, do you—the press, the loaded comments...the gossip?'

She hesitated. 'It's not in your nature to live a lie, Will. And that's what you have to do tonight. In the spotlight, in front of people you know...in front of friends. I think you're going to hate every moment of it.'

'I'll be there. It's what's expected of me. I won't let Carol Ann down.'

So they'd get to play the happy couple. Yippee. She'd need a soak in a hot bath before she could face that. And an aspirin.

All around him London's rich and wealthy—all the beautiful people—milled beneath the glittering chandeliers, smiling, air-kissing, dancing. It was all Will could do to not scowl.

If he received one more good-natured dig about being hog-tied and lassoed with his bachelor days far behind him, he might throw something.

He seized a glass of champagne from a passing tray—wished it were something stronger—and knocked it back in one. Across the room Sophie caught his eye and mouthed *smile*.

He forced the corners of his mouth upwards. He couldn't be too careful. With the press out in numbers tonight, you couldn't be certain who was watching. He couldn't let his guard down for a single moment. He winked and then blew her a kiss, and her lips twitched at what he guessed was the unexpectedness of it. A real smile lit through him. He liked surprising Sophie, liked taking her off guard…liked making her smile.

Not that he liked it too much. He ran a finger beneath the starched collar of his shirt. Her earlier words about her fear he was developing feelings for her knotted beneath his ribcage. He wasn't. Not a bit of it.

But she was Sophie, and that fact put her somehow apart from other women. Which meant his usual constraints weren't in place when he was around her.

That doesn't explain why you became so possessive of her.

He rolled his shoulders. As he'd said, there was a lot at stake.

'Will! Will!'

He nearly spilled his fresh champagne as Carol Ann came racing up and tugged on his arm. 'This is the most beautiful party I've ever been to!'

Her eyes sparkled, colour lit her cheeks, and she could barely keep still. 'It's pretty spectacular,' he agreed. 'Sophie sure knows how to throw a party. Want another spin around the dance floor?'

She shook her head. 'I want to watch for a little bit.'

It was clear that Sophie had lined up several young men to dance with his sister, and it touched him that she'd taken such pains to ensure Carol Ann had fun.

While news of his engagement had spread far and wide, Will noticed it didn't prevent women from sending him come-hither glances. He deliberately ignored them and did his best to forget the hog-tied comments that had him chafing as if he were on a leash. He wasn't hog-tied. He wasn't losing his freedom and independence. After the wedding he'd have the opportunity to follow some of those invitations to their logical conclusion. Discreetly, of course.

'Hello, Will, darling.'

'Simone, you're looking lovely this evening.' He and Simone had hooked up for a short while about a year ago. She'd left him in little doubt that she'd be more than happy to hook up with him again whenever he said the word.

'And you're as charming as ever. Aren't you going to ask me to dance?'

'Go away!' Carol Ann interjected, pushing in between Will and the other woman.

'Carol Ann, that's rude! Apologise at once.'

His sister pushed her lip out mutinously. 'You're not allowed to dance with anyone but Sophie.'

He blinked. 'I…uh… That's not exactly true, Carol Ann.' He turned to Simone. 'I'm sorry about my sister, she—'

'I love Sophie,' Carol Ann announced, too loudly.

Carol Ann loved everyone. But her face had

turned a blotchy red, and if he wasn't careful she'd create a god-awful scene.

'So does Will! Right, Will?'

His tie tightened about his neck, making it increasingly difficult to keep his breathing even. Simone raised an eyebrow and he wanted to flee. 'Of course I do.'

'How much?' Carol Ann demanded.

He searched his brain for a suitable answer. 'To the moon and back,' he finally growled.

His sister continued to glare at Simone. 'Then you shouldn't want to dance with anyone else!'

Instead of dissipating at his assurances, Carol Ann's distress seemed to grow. *Hell!* He didn't want the press getting pictures of Carol Ann blowing her top. It would be like reliving his childhood all over again. 'Carol Ann, you—'

'Hello, everyone, are you having a nice time?'

Sophie breezed up as if she hadn't a care in the world, and something inside him eased.

And then at the realisation his every muscle stiffened again.

'Ooh, Simone, your dress is divine. Is it an Alexander McQueen?'

Simone preened. 'It is. Like?'

'I'm absolutely pea-green.'

Carol Ann glared. 'She wanted to dance with Will.'

Sophie laughed. 'All the girls want to dance with Will. He's rather accomplished on the… dance floor.'

Her eyes danced as she made the strategic pause and he could feel his lips curve upwards, could feel himself falling under her spell.

'But—' she grinned at Carol Ann with such mischief that Carol Ann giggled '—they're not allowed to until he's danced with me first.'

With that she tugged him onto the dance floor and he had no choice but to slip an arm about her waist and draw her near, their bodies bumping together as they swayed to the music.

'Danger averted,' she murmured in his ear.

'Which danger? Carol Ann or Simone?'

She drew back, her eyes alive with laughter. It occurred to him that she really was in her element here in this glittering ballroom. 'Carol Ann, of course.'

'You're very good with her.' He should be happier about that. 'When did you get to read her so well?'

Like him she kept the smile on her lips, but it faded from the brilliant blue of her eyes. 'I've spent a lot of time with her this last fortnight.'

I love Sophie! Carol Ann's words went around and around in his head.

'She's becoming very attached to you.'

'I've become rather attached to her too. I'm not going to dump her when all of this is done, you know? Give me some credit. We'll remain friends. I'll still spend time with her, do things with her.'

Without him. Not that *that* mattered.

She squeezed his hands. 'Smile. One of the tabloid photographers has his sights set on us.'

He could do better than that.

The blood rushed through him as he pulled her firmly against him, twirled her before dipping her. She followed his lead effortlessly, not missing a beat. A huge smile curved her lips when he lifted her upright again, exhilaration spiking through her eyes and just for a moment he let that same exhilaration rush through him, let it slip all of his concerns from his shoulders until he felt free and light…and young.

Her head arced back in a laugh. 'You really are a demon on the dance floor.'

'And you really are stunning.'

She wore a blue satin cocktail dress that fitted her to perfection. It sported an intriguing

rectangular cut-out that ran beneath her col-
larbones and above her breasts, highlighting
the creamy perfection of her skin. He had to
fight the urge to bend her back over his arm
and press his lips to the skin there and taste
her. If she tasted half as good as she smelled
he'd be lost.

'Will.'

It wasn't a remonstration, but a whispered
breath filled with need. It had nothing to do
with them being friends and having this *arrangement*, or with her being Peter's sister. It
was a primal call between a man and a woman,
and he found himself powerless against the
forces battering him.

The music changed—turned slow and smoky.
He released her hand to curve both hands about
her waist to keep her so close their thighs and
hips touched. Their eyes locked in a stunned

and increasingly heated stare that should have steam rising in the air above them.

Everything else receded—the other couples on the dance floor, the band, the very room. With a boldness that felt just right, he pulled her hips in so close she couldn't mistake the effect she was having on him. Her breath hitched, and her lips parted as if she needed to drag air into oxygen-starved lungs.

Her hands rested against his chest, but one of them slid up around his shoulders to his nape and the contact fired every part of him that it touched with heat and life. He lowered his head until their breaths mingled.

This woman filled his senses—the look, feel and smell of her. He couldn't get enough.

He wanted her in his bed, naked. He wanted—

A flash went off, making them both jump.

Sophie recovered first. 'Enough,' she laughed with a wave of her hand to the photographer.

'Leave my fiancé and me in peace. Go and pick on someone else.'

Ice poured through him. Had she known all along that they were being photographed? Had she simply been playing it up for the cameras? Had she been faking…?

He dismissed that thought in the next moment when common sense caught up with him. She wanted him. He knew the signs and he saw how she tried to suppress that need. But it was clear she had more control of the situation than him.

He swore softly.

'Why are you upset?' she murmured. 'By the way, you're crushing my hand.'

He loosened his grip immediately with a terse apology.

'You played your part to perfection,' she added.

Her voice, though, wobbled, and he had to

swallow. No, she wasn't unaffected by him, but she wanted to be. And he'd promised her no complications.

Had he really been about to forget that and ask her to leave the party early? Had he really been about to ask her to come home with him? Had he really been about to break his word?

Acid burned through him.

Sophie remained in his arms, but she avoided his gaze and a respectable distance now separated them. 'You now have permission to dance with Simone.'

Her laugh grated down his spine, and his jaw tightened. 'I don't need your permission to dance with anyone.'

'I wasn't talking about my permission.' Her eyes snapped with a sudden fire. 'I was talking about Carol Ann's. Not only will she tell me all the names of who she danced with, but I don't doubt she'll tell me who you dance with too.'

Damn it! Sophie and Carol Ann were having a slumber party tonight. She'd never have come home with him!

What the hell had he been thinking?

He was getting too wrapped up in this woman. Their lives were becoming more and more entwined. He had to be careful not to take any of this too seriously. He couldn't let himself believe in the magic they were creating for the benefit of his grandfather.

It was a lie.

And even if beneath it all ran a thread of truth, he couldn't afford to let that thread have its head. He was determined that his heart remain free. He wasn't tying himself to a life of misery and manipulation, of anguish and grief. He'd never let a woman try to tear him to pieces the way his mother had done with his father. He would never do that to another person the way his father had with his mother.

He still sometimes woke in the middle of the night in a lather of sweat, recalling the screams, the fights, the tears. He wanted no part of any of that. He wasn't committing himself to any woman. He wasn't giving anyone that kind of power over him. He wanted peace, he wanted privacy, he wanted control—and if that made him selfish and an undutiful grandson then so be it. It was better than becoming a shell of a person, someone so damaged and defeated that they just gave up and didn't care if they lived or died. That was what a bad marriage could do to a person.

He and Sophie had a business arrangement. Nothing more. An arrangement that would end in eighteen months. His teeth ground together. As long as he maintained control, all would be well. Which would be easier with Sophie out of his arms, but for appearances' sake they had to continue with this farce of a dance.

'Carol Ann and I are going shopping tomorrow before heading back to Ashbarrow. Would you like to join us for lunch?'

He shook his head. 'I'm busy.' He'd make sure of it.

She stared at a point beyond his shoulder. 'I've been thinking… I don't think it's necessary to video conference every day now, do you? Maybe we can make it every other day?'

An impenetrable coldness washed through him. Sophie's primary motivation for being a part of this charade was money. He'd be a fool to forget it. 'I don't see there's any need for video conferencing at all now. We have everything under control. You can email me if anything goes wrong.'

She didn't blink, she didn't stiffen, nothing in her expression changed. 'Sounds like a plan.'

Sophie might be attracted to him, but she

wouldn't let an inconvenient attraction get in the way of a million pounds.

You're being unfair.

Maybe he was, but he suddenly felt like the world's biggest fool.

He released her the moment the song ended.

She immediately stepped away from him.

'I'll go and see if Simone is still interested in that dance.'

With a smile and a cheery wave she tossed a, 'Have fun,' over her shoulder before sauntering off, her high heels making the sway of her hips more pronounced. It was as if…as if she didn't have a care in the world.

A million pounds? His lips tightened. Maybe she didn't.

His jaw started to ache at how hard he clenched it. Well, he'd show her he hadn't a care in the world either. He'd prove it to the both of them.

* * *

'Hello, stranger.'

Will turned, a little unsteady on his legs, to find Simone leaning against one of the tall columns that marched down the steps of the hotel to the street. After his dance with Sophie, he hadn't hunted Simone down to see if she still wanted to dance. Instead he'd found a quiet corner and a waiter more than happy to keep his whisky glass filled.

He was going to have a hell of a head tomorrow. But for now he relished the warm hum that kept other unpleasantness at bay.

'Simone of the pretty dress!' If Sophie liked that dress so much it occurred to him now that he ought to buy her one.

He'd think about it tomorrow, because he'd promised himself to not think about Sophie for the rest of the evening.

Simone raised an eyebrow. She had pretty eyes but they were nothing to Sophie's.

'Don't tell me your fiancée has left you high and dry?'

He stumbled across to sit on the low wall beside her. 'She's thrown me over to have a slumber party with my little sister.'

Simone blinked. 'Well…that's nice.'

He nodded. And then he frowned. 'Yeah, it really is.' But then, Sophie was nice.

Simone stared at him and then gave a rueful laugh, though he didn't know why. 'Do you need a ride home, Will?'

'I do!' He rose to his feet, but everything spun so he sat again. 'That's what I came out for—to hail a cab.'

'My driver should be here any moment. Why don't I get him to give you a lift home?'

He thought about rising to his feet and trying to hail a cab, or remaining sitting here for a little while longer, and he chose the latter. 'You're a pal, Simone.'

'And here he is now. Come on, Will. On your feet.'

With a laugh he tossed an arm across her shoulders, and then found himself leaning a little too heavily on her. 'Sorry, I seem to have hit the whisky a little too hard.'

'Really?'

'You always were a good sport, Simone-of-the-pretty-dress.'

'Yay for me.' But she laughed as she said it. So Will laughed too and fell into the back of the car with her.

'Miss?' The driver turned to look at them.

'It's okay, Roberts.'

The world spun for a moment and Will had to take several deep breaths. 'Soph throws a damn fine party, doesn't she?'

'Indeed she does.'

He frowned. 'She looked so happy tonight—in her element—don't you think?'

Simone sighed. 'Absolutely.'

'So why would she want to open an equestrian centre when she'd be London's best party planner?'

Simone shook her head. 'And another one bites the dust.'

He frowned. What did she mean?

'Where to, miss?'

'We're dropping Mr Trent-Paterson home.'

The driver glanced into the rear-view mirror and said, 'I think it might be best if I drop you home first, miss.'

She nodded. 'I think that's an excellent plan.'

The moment Sophie entered the breakfast room at Ashbarrow Castle on Monday morning she knew something was wrong. She bit back a sigh. What was Lord Bramley up to now?

'Come and take a seat, Sophie.'

He'd started calling her Sophie since last Wednesday night, after he'd burst into her room in the mistaken belief he'd find Christian there. Finally his actions had shamed him. He'd been trying to make amends ever since. She had every intention of forgiving him, but not too quickly. She wanted him to understand that she wouldn't put up with that kind of behaviour.

'You look a little…serious.' Actually, he looked downright grim. She took the seat to his left. 'Don't tell me we're scheduled for another visit from Christian?'

His jowls worked. 'No, nothing like that. It's—'

He broke off and reached across to pat her hand. 'Now, my dear, I don't want you to fly off the handle or to get upset.'

Ice trickled down her neck, lodging in a hard

chill ball in her chest. What on earth had he done? 'You better just tell me whatever it is and get it over with.'

He turned grey.

She found herself suddenly clutching his hand. 'Dear God, it's Will, isn't it? Has he been hurt or—?'

'He's fighting fit.' The older man's lips twisted. 'Too fit, it seems.'

She dropped his hand as a different kind of chill settled over her. Without another word he turned the newspaper that was open in front of him towards her. She didn't want to look at it. She knew that with every cell of her body.

She held Lord Bramley's gaze until his dropped to the newspaper. Swallowing, she followed suit.

And flinched.

'Lass…'

She held up a hand and the older man fell silent as she took the paper and scanned the photographs. The first was of her and Will dancing, and she had to swallow at the raw sexuality that simmered between them—the intensity of their attraction evident for all to see. The second photograph was of Will with his arm about Simone, running down the front steps of the hotel towards a waiting car; they were both laughing.

He'd danced with her as he had, making every latent desire she'd ever had spring to life until it had been all she could do not to claw off his clothes and climb into his skin. She'd known he'd been doing it for the benefit of the cameras, but she'd also thought it had been true—that he'd felt as intensely as she had.

The edges of the newspaper crumpled as her fingers clenched. All of that *intensity*, it hadn't been for her alone. It was just *testosterone*. And it appeared that any available woman would do!

She shot to her feet. He was the one who'd

reminded her how high the stakes were. How could he have done such a stupid thing? How could he have done this…to her?

The captions read: Paradise Lost and Paradise Regained. She dropped the newspaper to the table and pressed a hand to her mouth, afraid she might be sick.

'Lassie, you need to sit and take a moment.'

There was a lot at stake. Too much. She forced her eyes wide. Forced air into lungs that didn't want to cooperate. 'There'll be an explanation for this. A perfectly innocent explanation.'

'Aye.'

But scepticism stretched through his eyes. How could Will have done this to her? She'd thought they were friends!

'I'm going for a ride.'

She wheeled from the room, ignoring Lord Bramley's entreaties for her to return.

'Saddle up Magnus,' she told Colin the moment she entered the stables.

He visibly swallowed. 'I'm sorry, Miss Mitchell, but Mr Will told me I wasn't to let you ride Magnus.'

Today Mr Will could go to hell. 'Then I'll saddle him myself.'

Still, she didn't want to get the groom into trouble. 'If it'll make you feel any better, you can saddle Annabelle and follow me.'

As soon as she had the big grey saddled, she swung up onto his back and cantered out of the yard, setting off towards the largest hill at a gallop, leaving Colin and Annabelle far behind. They galloped so fast she blamed the tears coursing down her cheeks on nothing more than the stinging wind in her face.

CHAPTER EIGHT

I T WAS THE helicopter that made Magnus become shy, grip the bit between his teeth and finally bolt.

Vaguely Sophie was aware of the machine landing in the forecourt of the castle ground, but most of her attention was taken up with Magnus and all the power hunched beneath her. She considered trying to bring the giant horse under control, but in the end she gave that up as a bad joke and just hung on.

Realising that she wasn't going to fight him, the horse relaxed his mouth, if not his speed, and she knew she could bring him to a halt if she wanted.

But she didn't want. She spurred him on instead.

They'd already been for a hard ride, but it hadn't been enough for Magnus. And it hadn't been enough for her either. She pushed him on hard—she wanted him thoroughly worn out. She wanted him to think twice before ever bolting on her again. His sides were heaving with exertion when she finally cantered him into the stable yard.

A grim-faced Will met her. He reached out and caught hold of the bridle, holding Magnus still while she slipped from his back.

'You could've been killed!'

The words emerged from between clenched teeth and Sophie found herself tossing her head, much as Magus had earlier. 'The only one in danger of being murdered today, Will, is you.'

Those lips whitened further. He turned his

head the merest fraction to glare at Colin. 'I told you she wasn't to ride Magnus.'

'There wasn't a whole lot he could do about it when I snuck into the stable and saddled Magnus myself.'

He glared at her. 'I could…'

She raised an eyebrow when he didn't finish. Throttle her? Good. That made them even.

She took the reins from Will's clenched hands and walked towards the stables. 'I need to give Magnus a good rub-down.'

Colin stepped forward. 'I can do that.'

She hesitated before handing over the reins. 'I'm sorry,' she murmured.

He shook his head. 'Don't be. It's not often we get to see such expert horsemanship. It was a bit of a treat, to be honest.'

She could feel Will's glower from where she stood, and Colin made a hasty exit with Magnus. She watched them go and wondered if she could poach Colin for her equestrian centre.

The next moment her arm was gripped by unrelenting fingers and she found herself marched away from the castle, away from all the outbuildings, and in the direction of a copse of trees. She knew from previous exploration that a clear sweet stream flowed down there.

'You could've broken your neck!'

She pulled free from his grasp. 'So could you!' She pointed towards the helicopter.

'That is a safe mode of transportation!'

'While I was never in any danger!'

They were both breathing hard and her legs were shaking. It was delayed reaction from the wild ride. It had absolutely nothing to do with the bristling display of masculinity in front of her. At least that was what she told herself. 'You're such an idiot, Will.'

They both knew she no longer referred to horses or helicopters.

'I don't want to have this conversation where anyone can see us.'

He went to take her arm again but she wouldn't let him. She leaned forward to poke him in the chest. Beneath her finger his muscles were bunched tight and hard. 'You were the one who told me how high the stakes were on Saturday night.' She kept her voice low, making sure it carried no further than Will's ears. 'And yet you were the one who went home with another woman. At a ball your fiancée was hosting…and where said fiancée was taking such pains to ensure your sister enjoyed herself so much she couldn't wait to come back to London. So that she'd no longer fear London but would start to associate it with fun and joy. And you—'

She couldn't finish the sentence. She'd never expected his fidelity, but she'd thought he'd…

She thought he'd treat her with respect.

Evidently she'd been wrong.

He bent at the waist, bracing his hands on his knees. 'Sophie—'

She pushed against his shoulder, though it barely made an impression on him. Still, he turned his head to meet her gaze. 'Do you think Peter would pat you on the back for this…tell you what a good guy you are?' She shook her head and then flung an arm towards the hill she and Magnus had just climbed. 'He'd take you out there and beat the crap out of you.'

'And I'd let him.' He straightened, his face white and his breathing coming hard and sharp.

She wheeled away, heading for the trees and stream. 'You needn't think that makes a scrap of difference.'

In two strides he'd caught up with her, his

hands on her shoulders pulling her to a halt. 'Nothing happened.'

'Let go of me.'

He dropped his hands immediately. 'Nothing happened,' he repeated.

'Wow!' She folded her arms. 'You've never lied to me before. You must be feeling *really* guilty.'

His nostrils flared. 'I'm not lying to you now.'

She went to turn away.

'I did not sleep with Simone.'

She halted.

'I got stupid drunk and she gave me a lift home. End of story. I rang her yesterday to apologise for the state I was in and for putting her driver to so much trouble.'

'Why didn't you ring me as well?'

'Because there was nothing to tell! I didn't know the papers were going to run with the stupid story.'

Given he was a successful businessman, he must have a great poker face, but…

She wanted to believe him. How much frightened her.

'For God's sake, Sophie, give me some credit! You know how much I hate a fuss or spectacle in the newspapers. If I'd had my sights set on Simone I'd have slipped out with her far more discreetly than that.'

He had a point, but…

'Simone is a good sport. She'd been considering a final fling with me.'

That didn't make her a good sport! It made her a—

'But not once she realised how drunk I was.' He grimaced. 'Apparently all I could talk about was you anyway. So she gave me up for a lost cause.'

'Me? You talked about me?'

He raked a hand back through his hair. 'According to her I extolled your many virtues.'

'Oh, now I really don't believe you.' But she did. And she could tell that, from her tone of voice, he knew it too.

'I'm going to be brutally honest now.' They'd reached the shade of the trees and Will shoved his shoulders back. The sound of the stream splashed and burbled in the still air. 'I got so drunk on Saturday night because I was going out of my mind with lust for you. I want you like I can't remember wanting any woman.'

'No!' She took a step backwards when all she wanted to do was hurl herself into his arms.

He cocked an eyebrow. 'Denying it doesn't make it any the less true.'

She twisted her hands together. 'It's only because we've put…limits on our relationship. If they weren't there I wouldn't seem half so attractive to you.'

'I wish I could believe that.' He dragged in a breath that made him grow taller. 'But I made you a promise.'

Her heart raced and her stomach churned. 'And it's one that I'm going to hold you to.'

'Why?'

The single word cracked from between white lips. What did he mean, *why*?

He leaned forward and took her chin between gentle but inexorable fingers. 'I could make you feel so good, Sophie Mitchell. I'd work so hard at it, apply myself so assiduously, that I'd make you scream—' his voice lowered '—with pleasure…and then I'd make you purr. And I'd do it again and again and again.'

Her mouth went dry with longing. 'Stop it!' She pressed her fingers to his mouth and tried to fight the tempting breeze that shimmered across the surface of her skin, tightening her nipples to hard, aching buds.

'Why not, Sophie? We'd be good together and you know it.'

Because the stakes were too high—her heart, this strange friendship of theirs...their shared memories of Peter. Not to mention the far from simple matter that she'd sworn to turn over a new leaf. She wasn't risking all of that. 'Because you don't do love and commitment, and I no longer use sex as a tool to...to forget.'

He let go of her as if she'd burned him.

She gestured. 'Let's go down to the stream.'

Once down at the stream, Sophie sat on a rock and Will stood with his back to her and started skimming stones at a spot where the stream widened and formed a calm pool. Her heart throbbed and no amount of deep breathing or swallowing eased it. 'You could call the wedding off, you know, Will.'

He spun around. 'No! Why would you even suggest that?'

'Call it a stab in the dark, but… Because you don't want to be married?'

He dismissed that with a snort and a wave of his hand.

'And because with a little effort on your part I believe you could reconcile Carol Ann to living in London with you. I'd help.'

He raised an eyebrow. 'For a fee?'

'Don't be ridiculous! Are you trying to deliberately rile me? We wouldn't be fiancés, but we'd still be friends.' Wouldn't they? Her heart started to pound. It was why she couldn't sleep with him. It was why she had to transform the idea from an alluring temptation for him to a potential nightmare instead. 'You know I wouldn't do it for money.'

She'd do it because she cared about Will and Carol Ann. She'd do it because it was what Peter would've wanted her to do.

One thing Peter most certainly would've

counselled her against was getting involved in a physical relationship with his best friend.

He dragged both hands back through his hair and nodded. 'I know. I'm sorry.'

He came and sat on the ground, his back resting against her rock. 'My feelings for this place—' he gestured out in front of them '—are complicated, Sophie. After the life Carol Ann and I had with our parents this was…a haven.'

Living with his parents had been a constant roller-coaster ride of anxiety and insecurity. And all of it lived in the glare of the public spotlight. No wonder he hated appearing in the society pages now. It made Saturday night's exploits all the more extraordinary. Usually he was so careful.

She stared out at the rolling deep green fields, the clear brook and the blue of the sky. 'This must've seemed like an idyll after London.'

'Some days it still does,' he admitted. 'If you can discount my grandfather, which evidently I can't. But back then… I don't know. I could walk, run, ride. I could go for a swim.'

She imagined him in nothing but a pair of brief swim trunks and heat flooded her cheeks. It was all she could do not to fan herself.

'I could do all of those things—normal things—without having reporters shoving microphones under my nose or having to dodge camera flashes every time I left the house. It was such a *relief.*'

Her heart went out to the boy who'd had to live his life in such a public fishbowl.

'This place was freedom and security. I'd never had those things before.'

And finally she saw what he refused to admit even to himself. Ashbarrow Castle was the home of his heart. Despite the successful and autonomous life he'd created for himself in

London, this was where his soul craved to be. He wanted to keep it safe for Carol Ann, yes. But he wanted to keep it safe for himself too. Her eyes started to sting and she had to blink hard.

'Unfortunately, the moment I turned fourteen this place became a prison.'

Which was all due to his grandfather's attempts to control him. Why was Lord Bramley so unbending, rigid…determined to force Will into a course of action that was such anathema to him? It was as if the older man wanted to punish him. And yet, that didn't make sense, didn't quite ring true.

'I believe you about Carol Ann—especially after seeing her having such a good time on Saturday night. I probably could help her make the transition to living in London, but…'

He frowned and all his shoulder muscles tightened. It took all the strength she possessed to stop from reaching out and running her hand through his dark, auburn-tinted hair. 'But?'

His gaze swung around to meet hers. 'Ashbarrow has always been a haven for her—never a prison. She loves it. It's her home, and it's not fair that she should be asked to give it up.'

She pulled in a breath and then let it out slowly, a weight pressing down on her. 'You're right. It wouldn't be fair.' Life wasn't fair, but Carol Ann had already had her share of unfairness. So had Will. After the trauma and upheaval of their early years, they deserved to keep their home. Both of them.

'Sophie, I'm sorry I was such a total idiot on Saturday night. I'm sorry I made it look as if I'd been unfaithful to you.' He rose to sit beside her. 'I'm sorry I hurt you.'

She tried to shrug away the warmth that

wanted to wrap about her. 'Look, Will, you never promised me your fidelity. I don't expect it.'

'But I did promise you friendship and discretion.' He was silent for a moment. 'I should've been careful not to set tongues wagging. I should've been on my guard, and not allowed a fit of pique to jeopardise everything.'

Her eyebrows rose. What had he called it? 'A fit of pique?'

His face darkened. 'You and Carol Ann were having so much fun—you'd been shopping, you were having a slumber party and I felt like the third wheel. I was...*jealous*.'

'You big baby!'

'That's fair.' He nodded. 'And I've been called worse.' He sobered. 'I promise it won't happen again.'

Good.

He glanced at her from the corner of his eye. She stiffened. 'What?'

'I didn't realise you were promising me *your* fidelity.'

She swallowed. 'Who said I was?'

'I no longer use sex as a tool to forget.'

She shot to her feet and strode to the edge of the stream. 'I'm not promising it to you. I'm promising it to myself.' She was determined to leave the party lifestyle behind her.

'You're allowed to have sex just for fun, Sophie.'

His voice came from just behind her and it took all her strength not to turn. 'I've been having a bit too much fun these last couple of years. I want to focus on other things.' Like helping Carla. Like building up something that belonged just to her. 'I want to find some balance in my life.'

'Good for you.'

Which was odd when she was standing here feeling more unbalanced than she ever had in her life before.

'So…we're good?'

She turned. 'We're good.'

He stood too close and it made her throat hitch and her mouth go dry. He bent and pressed a warm kiss to her cheek, and her heart pounded so hard she thought he must hear it.

'Except,' she pushed out from an uncooperative throat.

He'd taken a step away, but he froze now and she could see how his every muscle bunched. 'Except?'

'I want you to talk to your grandfather. Today.'

Will's every muscle screamed a protest. He wanted to shout a resounding No! until the sound of it rang through the hills.

He still couldn't believe he'd been stupid enough, careless enough, to create a media brouhaha that had allowed the tabloids to make any number of impertinent and unsavoury claims about his relationship with Sophie. He who hated any kind of media acknowledgement—even plaudits for his business acumen and the success of Pyxis Tech.

Sophie deserved better from him. She sure as hell didn't deserve him yelling at her now.

He forced himself to turn and meet her gaze. Was she really willing to forgo her million pounds so he could avoid a marriage he didn't want? He had a feeling that the answer to that question was an unhesitating yes. *Damn it!* He nodded. 'Okay.'

Her shoulders loosened and she let out a shuddering breath, the beginnings of a smile playing across her lips. 'Good.'

He wanted her to have her million pounds.

He wanted her to have the chance to follow her dreams. And he wanted her to know how much he appreciated her.

If he could, he'd like to wipe away all the hurt he'd caused her. She'd felt betrayed—not romantically, but that didn't make the betrayal any the less painful. He understood that.

'I couldn't do this with any other woman, Sophie. I want you to know I appreciate all you've taken on, all you're doing. You've earned your million pounds several times over.'

Her eyes narrowed. 'Don't even think of offering me any more money.'

Why the hell not?

'And I think you're underestimating some of the women you know.'

He shook his head. On this point at least he was certain. 'No other woman knows me as well as you do.'

Those eyes widened and he lost himself in

the clearness of that blue for a moment. She shrugged. 'We've known each other a long time, Will.'

'I keep women at arm's length.'

She snorted and picked up a stone and tried to skim it across the stream, but her technique was all wrong and it sank like a…uh…stone. 'That's not what I hear.'

He winced. 'I mean emotionally. I keep them—'

'I knew what you meant.'

A hint of laughter lit her eyes, making them sparkle like this stream in the sun at midday. How had he never clocked the many expressions in her eyes before? They were utterly fascinating.

'Well, I don't do that with you.'

She stilled and then shook her head. 'You would if we slept together.'

Would he?

She turned so they faced each other fully, hands on her hips. 'It's the same for me, you know? I'm more emotionally vulnerable to you than I am to any other man.'

Emotionally vulnerable? Was that what he'd been describing? He supposed it was, but, rather than feeling emotionally exposed, with Sophie it felt comfortable...comforting even.

'Does it frighten you?'

His head rocked back. 'No! I trust you.' She'd never try to manipulate him. 'I value the person you are. I think you feel the same about me.'

She nodded.

A new thought—one that appalled him—rippled through him. 'Does it frighten you?'

She met his gaze, swallowed and nodded.

A vice tightened about his temples. 'Why?'

She turned and started back towards the castle. She stopped before they cleared the copse of trees. Shadows played across her face, making it difficult to read. 'Why?' he repeated. He hated the thought that anything about him frightened her.

'Because I'm attracted to you, Will. Because I want you.'

Roaring in his ears shut out every other sound. He had to swallow hard to quieten it to a manageable din. His mouth dried. 'But you said…'

'We're not going to sleep together. If we do you'll become more emotionally distant while I'd be in danger of become more—' her fingers grasped the air as if searching for the right word '—emotionally invested.'

He took a step back, shock rocketing through him when he finally realised what she'd been trying to tell him. Sometimes sex meant nothing, but sometimes it meant everything. And he knew that because he always ended his ro-

mantic liaisons before sex meant even a potential something. Sophie didn't have any of
the usual barriers where he was concerned. If
he slept with her, he'd be in danger of breaking her heart.

He couldn't do that!

He raked a hand back through his hair. 'Complicated,' he murmured, recalling her warning
the first night they'd spent here at Ashbarrow.

She nodded. 'C'mon, it's time we returned
to the house.'

Returning to face his grandfather suddenly
didn't seem anywhere near as intimidating as
it had a moment or two ago.

'You should—'

He took her hand. He wanted to squeeze it
to tell her how sorry he was that he'd been so
obtuse earlier, that he'd forced her to spell it
out for him in detail. 'I should?'

She laughed. 'Hold my hand for the benefit

of all the noses currently pressed against the castle windows. But I can see you were ahead of me.'

To hell with watching eyes! 'Can I raise another topic in relation to Saturday night?'

She glanced at him. 'Go on.'

'You.'

'Me?'

'You were in your element hosting that party. You really seemed to enjoy yourself.'

'I was seeing off my last commitment to my father. It was…satisfying.'

Had he misread the situation? A moment later he shook his head. 'I think you enjoyed the party.'

She opened her mouth as if to deny his words, and then her shoulders sagged. 'I did,' she said, as if it were the worst thing in the world to confess. 'I'm the shallowest creature on the face of the planet—I love parties.'

He pulled her to a halt. 'That doesn't make you shallow. It makes you a people person. You did a brilliant job on Saturday night—you made sure everyone had a great time. You not only helped to raise a ridiculous sum of money for charity, but you were instrumental in encouraging the guests to open their wallets so widely. That isn't shallow.'

She stared at him, unconvinced.

He lifted their linked hands to point a finger at her. 'You did nothing to be ashamed of on Saturday night.' That'd been his domain. 'You think I didn't notice that while you were never without a flute of champagne in your hand, you never took so much as a sip?'

Her mouth dropped open.

'Do you think I didn't notice that the young men you had lined up to dance with Carol Ann were the kind of young men who'd enjoy her company too?

'And you dealt with Lord Graham—' a notorious drunk '—without fuss or drawing attention to him.' She'd packed him off home in a cab before he'd managed to disgrace himself or his wife. 'You should be proud of yourself, Sophie.'

She moistened her lips, an unfamiliar vulnerability shining out from her eyes, and for a moment he felt unaccountably honoured that she didn't try to hide it from him. 'Do you really think so?'

'I know so.'

Before he thought of the wisdom of it, he bent down to press his lips gently to hers, telling her without words that he thought she was wonderful. Their lips held, clung, and then he forced himself upright.

'Believe me?'

'I… I guess.' With her free hand she tucked a stray strand of hair behind her ear.

He turned them back towards the castle. 'Which begs the question... If you love event planning so much, why aren't you pursuing a career in that? I know you want to look after Carla, but there are other ways to do it. You don't have to go to the trouble and expense of setting up an equestrian centre.'

She was silent for a long moment. 'I've pretty much squandered my entire trust fund and inheritance, other than that bit of property in Cornwall. I want to do something *good* with it, something worthwhile. And I think you'll understand it when I say I'd like to have something that's just mine. Something that I built and created.'

He did understand that.

'Something to fall back on if I ever need to.'

She could fall back on him whenever she needed.

'I don't want to manage an equestrian centre forever. I'm hoping that, down the track, it's something Carla would like to do. But in the meantime I can't wait to get started on it. It excites me so much.'

The truth of that shone from her eyes.

'I wonder if maybe I couldn't find a way to do both things—run the equestrian centre *and* event plan.'

'Of course you could. You're smart, talented, energetic and amazing. I don't doubt for a single moment that you could achieve anything you set your mind to.'

With a laugh, she bumped his shoulder with hers. 'Careful or you'll be in danger of turning my head.'

He grinned. Flattery was not the way to her heart. He knew that. They were both safe. But it was good to hear her laugh again.

His grandfather was waiting for them the

moment they crossed the threshold. 'I want to speak to you in my study, young man. *Now!*'

'Have fun,' Sophie murmured under her breath. 'Come find me on the terrace when you're done.'

He dropped a kiss to the top of her head and then turned to his grandfather. 'That's fortuitous because I want to talk to you too.'

Thirty minutes later Will slammed himself into the chair opposite Sophie's—one with a view of green fields and that babbling brook of a stream. She had a view of the castle, and she'd seen him coming—her gaze had felt like a physical presence on his flesh—but he hadn't meant to slam himself with quite so much force to the chair. She winced and he grimaced. 'Sorry.'

She shook her head, all that abundant blond hair fanning about her shoulders. 'It looks as if perhaps I should be the one apologising to you. I thought talking to your grandfather would help.'

He appreciated her optimism, but...

She leaned forward. 'I thought it would give you some answers.'

He held back a harsh laugh. 'Oh, it did that.'

She halted halfway through pouring him a cup of tea, her perfect lips forming a perfect O. With a shake of her head she continued pouring the tea, cut him a luscious slice of chocolate cake and set both in front of him. As delicious as the tea looked it was nothing to her lips.

Her lips are off-limits.

He took a sip of tea. He took a bite of cake. But neither eased the burn in his soul. 'You know, when I was little—before my parents died—my grandfather was my hero.'

The blue of her eyes deepened to the colour of the ocean. 'He was?'

'He'd sweep in during the holidays and bring me and Carol Ann up here for as long as he could get away with. It was a respite from the chaos of living with my parents.'

'I wonder that they didn't simply leave you both with him.' The moment the words left her, her hand flew to her mouth. 'Oh, I don't mean they didn't love you and Carol Ann, it's just…' She grimaced. 'I think I better quit before I dig myself a deeper hole.'

He laughed and took pity on her. 'My parents weren't interested in parenting. I think we can agree on that much.'

She nodded, her eyes shadowed.

'But they were interested in displaying the accessories of family life that would garner them as much media attention as possible. The tabloids lap up pictures of celebrities with their kids.' He could feel his lips twist, saw the way her gaze flicked to them, lingered, before she glanced away again, and it took a force of effort to keep his breathing even. 'And they love stories about celebrities behaving badly and having sordid affairs with nannies and pool boys even more.'

She rubbed her fingers across her forehead as if trying to push back a headache. He sympathised. His parents had always been headache-inducing.

He bit into the cake, munched and pondered. 'I think my father enjoyed punishing my grandfather.'

She nodded as if his words made complete sense. Which shouldn't be surprising, he supposed, but as far as he was concerned his parents had never made any sense whatsoever.

'But here's what I never realised—my grandfather blames himself for my father's wild lifestyle. He says he wasn't strict enough when my father was growing up, that he spoiled him and went too easy on him, didn't keep him on a tight enough rein. He believes that's the reason my father went so completely off the rails. As a result he's determined not to make the same mistake with me.'

She clapped a hand to her head. 'Oh, that makes perfect sense!'

It did.

She frowned. 'Except…you're not fourteen years old any more but a grown man.'

His point exactly.

She seized her cup and took a gulp as if she needed the sustenance.

Will's insides twisted. 'He claims I'm a chip off the old block—that I'm as bad as my father.'

She'd started to choke as if her tea had gone down the wrong way and he went to slap her on the back, but she pointed behind him. He turned to find his grandfather standing there, all bristling aggression.

'You *will* learn to toe the line, William, and to curb your reprehensible behaviour and degraded way of life, *or* there will be consequences as you'll learn to your detriment.'

The table rattled and Will turned to find that Sophie had shot to her feet. Her hands had clenched to fists and she literally shook.

She looked magnificent!

'Lord Bramley, you're mistaken! And in danger of sounding like a fool because only a fool would consider Will and all he's achieved as bad, reprehensible or degraded. He's built an unbelievably successful business empire entirely through his own ingenuity and sheer hard work, but do you pat him on the back and tell him how proud you are of him? No! *What is wrong with you?'*

In her frustration she shouted the words so loud Will thought the entire valley would hear her.

His grandfather started rumbling something about duty and what Will owed his family name, but she wouldn't let him continue.

'He is not his father! Will doesn't do drugs. He doesn't lie, cheat or steal.'

'He's a womaniser!'

'He only has affairs with women who are willing! He doesn't have affairs with married women. He doesn't use his position as the boss to chat up junior members of staff. He doesn't sexually harass women. He rarely drinks to excess, he mostly stays out of the tabloids—even given who he is and his family history.'

'But—'

'No buts! He's a man who's doing something productive and useful with his life.'

'But—'

'And you should love him for who he is rather than trying to force him into a carbon copy of you.'

For a moment the only sound was the twittering of birds in the nearby hedge, and Sophie's ragged breathing.

'You want him to love this place, you want to bind him to it, but all you've done is turn the one place in this world that he considered home into a prison.'

Her voice had quietened, but it was all the more deadly for it. She lifted her chin. 'Given what happened to your son, I can understand why you're a mass of insecurities.' She blinked as if something startling had just occurred to her. She moistened her lips, her mind racing behind the blue of her eyes. With a shake, she set her shoulders again. 'But nobody else can shore up your insecurities for you, except you.

Asking and demanding that someone else do that for you isn't just pointless, it...it's unfair.'

She stared at both men with stunned blue eyes. 'It isn't fair,' she repeated. Before Will could say anything, she'd taken off for the house and disappeared inside the depths of the castle.

Will went to go after her, but his grandfather's hand on his arm stayed him. 'Do you consider this place home?'

'I did. Once.'

And then he shook off the older man's hand and set off after Sophie.

CHAPTER NINE

SOPHIE KNEW THE exact moment Will entered their shared sitting room, sensed that he stood in the doorway and watched her to try and decipher her mood.

But, for the moment, she couldn't control her pacing. The best she could manage was to toss an, 'I'm sorry,' over her shoulder to him.

Again, she sensed rather than saw him move a little farther into the room. 'You have nothing to apologise for. I… I loved what you said to my grandfather just now. Nobody has ever defended me like that before.'

That managed to still her. She turned, folding her hands at her waist. The warmth of his smile, the affection in his eyes increased the ache in her chest. 'Oh, Will, I'm not apologising about that.' It was well beyond time that somebody took Lord Bramley to task for his attitude to Will. For all the good it had done. She started to pace again.

'Then what are you apologising for?'

Another glance at him had her wanting to cover her face with her hands. 'Because, in my own way, I've been as bad as your grandfather.'

His face darkened and his stance widened as he pointed a finger at her. 'That's not true.'

Yes, it was. 'I've been using you to keep Peter's memory alive. I've forced you into a role that you've hated, all because… All because I've been afraid that everyone would forget him.' She pressed her palms to her eyes. 'Because I've been afraid that I'd forget him.' And because she'd felt guilty—guilty that she was alive when he wasn't. Guilty for enjoying all the things she'd once enjoyed—and for enjoying new things—when he wasn't here to enjoy them too.

She'd clutched her grief and her memories to her tightly so as to keep her brother's memory fresh and alive, refusing to move on—and refusing to let either Will or Carla move on either.

It had been spectacularly unfair.

She dragged her hands away. 'I'm sorry I've forced you into a role that you didn't want and that you didn't ask for. I'm sorry I tried to turn you into a substitute for Peter. I've been trying to shore up my own grief and fears, just like your grandfather. Only I didn't see that until I accused him of it just now.'

In three strides he was in front of her. He took her hands, making her pulse skitter and start. 'Sophie, you've not forced me into anything. Watching you grieve these past two years has been hard. I've wanted to do whatever I could to ease your pain, but I've had to face the fact that it's the one thing I couldn't do.'

'Oh! So I've made you feel like a failure too!'

She tried to tug her hands away, but he wouldn't let her go. 'Not a failure, Sophie, just…human. You've kept me human. Through all of this.'

Her heart stopped and then gave a gigantic kick, and she found herself clutching his hands in an effort to keep her balance. 'You—' She had to swallow the lump in her throat. 'You've always been human, Will. You're one of the kindest people I know.'

He shook his head. 'I've tried to be kind to you. Always. From that first day I met you I knew your parents had hurt you in some way… in a similar way that my parents had hurt me.'

Her throat thickened and her eyes stung.

His grip tightened. 'My parents, and to a certain extent my grandfather, have left me with a burning desire to succeed and to never be vulnerable to anyone again. Carol Ann, Peter and you are the only ones I've let myself care about. When Peter died I was in danger of closing myself off completely—of becoming a robot. But, Sophie, our monthly coffee dates wouldn't let me put my heart on ice. It's only just occurred to me but you made me keep feeling, and while a part of me resented it, another part of me realises it was a gift.

'So.' He lifted one of her hands and pressed his lips to her knuckles. 'Don't ever apologise to me for your grief or for the past two years, because you've helped me more than you've harmed me.'

She couldn't speak. All she could do was stare at him.

'Say something,' he finally begged.

She pulled her hands free from his and he

let them go. She had to take a few steps away from him and his dark lime scent to gather her scattered thoughts. From the window she saw Lord Bramley and Carol Ann tramping across the fields.

She swung back to Will. 'Everything feels different now,' she blurted out.

He pursed those divine lips and leant towards her. A flush of heat shot through her. 'Good different or bad different?'

She considered that for a moment. 'I don't know.' She lifted a shoulder and then let it drop. The weight that had been pressing down on her had lifted. 'I feel…lighter, freer.'

'That's *good* different.'

She lifted her chin and stared at him, openly admired the broad sweep of his shoulders and the athletic strength of his legs. She took in the dark glint of his hair and the firm promise of his lips. 'When I look at you now I no longer see Peter.' A sense of loss accompanied that, but it was a good difference too. Will was his own man. He deserved better than to be defined by a ghost.

His eyes darkened and the pulse at the base of his throat pounded. 'What do you see?'

'I see all the things you are to me. I see *our* friendship now.'

He swallowed and nodded. She glanced at that pulse in his throat and knew he was fighting the same desire that flooded her.

'I see a man so potently attractive it's all I can do to not fling myself at him.'

The confession should frighten her, but it didn't.

Will's quick intake of breath and the way his nostrils flared were the only signs that betrayed her words had any effect on him. *'Sophie.'*

She ignored the warning in his voice.

'I've used Peter as an excuse to hide from the attraction I feel for you too…used it to keep you at arm's length. I've basically emotionally blackmailed you into not sleeping with me.'

'That's garbage! It's—'

'Is it?'

He broke off, his eyes burning into hers, and all she wanted to do was kiss him and feel those hands on her body.

'I let you think that if anything happened to our friendship, I wouldn't be able to cope. I let you think it'd be like losing Peter all over again.' She had to swallow. 'But finally I've realised that my love for Peter and the memories I have of him don't depend on you or Carla or anyone else. Peter lives on in my heart and there's nothing that can remove him. So whether we continue to fight our attraction or give into it, Will, it'll have no effect on how I feel about my brother.'

His eyes glittered and he held himself un-naturally still. 'Why are you telling me this?'

'And that's definitely a good change,' she added, not answering his question.

She moved across to where he stood, reached out and placed her hand over his heart. His warmth and the steady beat beneath her palm made her feel free. 'I'm tired of lying—to my-self and to you. I don't want to fight what I feel for you any more. It's a long time since I did something I wanted just for me.'

The pounding beneath her palm grew harder and stronger.

'And just so we're clear on this, I'm not after love and commitment, white picket fences and children. I know you don't want to be tied down and I'd never try to do that to you.'

'So what are you after?'

She could feel her lips curve upwards and her eyes start to dance. She threw her head back provocatively to stare him full in the face. 'Pleasure,' she said boldly. 'Physical release and pleasure.'

His hands gripped her shoulders and while they were gentle against her flesh, she could feel their latent strength. They silently narrated the battle raging through him. He didn't know whether to hold her or shake her—whether to pull her to him or thrust her away.

'You said if we slept together it'd become complicated.'

And yet now it seemed incredibly simple. 'It'll only become complicated if we're not honest with each other. We're friends, yes?'

He gave a hard nod.

'This is just going to be a fling, right? We're not doing anything long-term. Eventually it'll burn itself out, and when it does we call it a day with no hard feelings. And we remain friends.'

He moved in closer until their chests touched. Heat spiked through her and her nipples hardened to tight aching buds. *Kiss me. Kiss me. Kiss me.* The plea sounded through her but she didn't utter it out loud. She had a feeling he could see it shining from her eyes.

'Can you do that?'

The words grated from him and she could tell he was holding on to his control by only a thread. 'I can. I have no unrealistic expectations of you or myself. Can you?'

Those firm lips lifted upwards into a hungry, wolfish smile. 'It's my speciality.'

And then his hands lowered to her hips and he pulled her hard up against him, leaving her in no doubt of his desire for her; she sucked in a breath and tried to keep her balance. His fingers curved into the flesh of her backside and stars burst behind her eyelids.

She gripped his waist to steady herself. 'This

is all completely separate from our marriage arrangement. That's business and this is…'

He stilled. 'This is?'

'It's something completely different. It's just for us. Because we want to. And for no other reason.'

His hand curved about the back of her head to cradle it, to hold it still while he explored the shape of her jaw with his other hand, tracing the outline of her bottom lip with his thumb.

Her breathing grew ragged. 'Stop tormenting me, Will, and kiss me.'

His lips curved upwards. 'Whatever the lady wants.' And then his mouth lowered and his lips touched her, sparking heat and need. He kissed her with a thoroughness that made her tremble, that made her want to crawl inside him. She wanted more, so much more.

Her tongue tangled with his and she gave up wrestling with the buttons on his shirt to pull it free from the waistband of his trousers instead, her breath hissing out when she finally made skin-on-skin contact. He felt firm and silken beneath her palms and she gloried in the way he shivered when she raked her fingernails lightly across his bare skin.

In the next moment she found herself pressed firmly against the wall behind her and her hands captured and held above her head. Will pressed lazy kisses along her jaw to her neck, each and every one of them sparking sensation through her. She moved against him restlessly. 'What are you doing?' she panted.

Dark eyes met hers and the intent in them melted her bones. If he hadn't been holding her up she'd have fallen in a heap. 'I've waited a long time for this moment, Sophie, and I've no intention of rushing it.'

Her pulse went off the chart. 'Not even if I were to beg?'

Was that her voice? She swallowed. 'I mean for this fling to last beyond one encounter, Will.' She tugged and he released her hands. She fisted them in the front of his shirt and pulled his head down to hers. 'I want you *now*! Slow and leisurely can wait until later tonight.'

And then she kissed him with all the fire in her soul, and her soul could've sung when the final thread of his control snapped and he kissed her back with just as much hunger and just as much need.

Sophie turned her head from where it rested beside Will's on the pillow. She hadn't curled up against his side. He hadn't flung an arm across her waist. But their hands were clasped on the bed between them, their fingers interlaced. 'Just…wow!' she breathed.

He turned to meet her gaze, a grin stretching across his face. 'I couldn't have put it more eloquently myself.'

'This isn't feeling awkward for me. What about you?'

He shook his head. 'Regrets?'

'Uh huh.' She nodded. 'One huge one—that it took me so long to sort out how I really felt about everything. We could've been doing this for weeks!'

His rumble of laughter vibrated through her, warming her to the soles of her feet. And then, before she realised what he was about, he'd rolled her under him and every part of her quickened in response.

'There's nothing like making up for lost time,' he murmured, his teeth gently tugging on her earlobe.

Pleasure spiked through her and she arched beneath him, glorying in his weight and the sparks of heat that shot through her wherever they touched. 'Very true—making up for lost time could become my new mantra over the next couple of weeks.' She gasped, running her hands down his sides and relishing the way it made him quiver. 'Tell me you don't need to rush back to London today.'

'I may never go back to London again,' he murmured against her lips, before capturing them in a kiss that hurled them both back into a maelstrom of pleasure and desire.

Three days later, Sophie wondered if that grip would ever ease. She'd had good sex before, but what she shared with Will wasn't just good. It was *spectacular*. She hadn't known it could be like this.

Not that she said that to Will, of course. It smacked too much of a neediness that would send him running for the hills. She didn't want him running for the hills. Not yet.

Not that they spent all their time in bed. They spent hours on Magnus and Annabelle as he showed her all the places he'd loved when he was young. They explored the glens and the hills, traversed lochs and cantered through crystal-clear streams. They spent hours playing board games and watching musicals with Carol Ann.

But when they retired to their room each night—they made love as if they never wanted to stop. Not just once, but again and again. As if they couldn't get enough of each other. As if they were addicted.

It wasn't until Thursday, though, that Sophie finally realised how much trouble she was in. When Will told her he had to go back to London the next day. The depth of the protest that rose through her had her clutching the wedding folder she held to her chest. As casually as she could, she leant a shoulder against the bedroom doorframe to counter the sensation of falling, of dizziness. Loss, anguish and despair all pounded through her.

Will sat on the side of the bed, his back to her, pulling on his shoes, so she allowed herself precisely three seconds to close her eyes and drag in a breath, to pull herself together. 'No rest for the wicked?' she forced herself to ask, with award-winning composure.

He didn't move and she tried to paste what she hoped was a cheeky grin into place. 'I suppose I should be focusing on the wedding anyway. Nine days, Will. The month has flown!'

He turned, a frown in his eyes. 'Do you want to back out?'

'Of course not.' It was just... She hadn't known when she'd agreed to this paper marriage that she'd be marrying the man she *loved*. 'Do you?'

He shook his head. 'I'm determined to safeguard Carol Ann's future, but...'

'But?' she echoed from her spot in the door-way. She couldn't move, not a single muscle. Those ruthless eyes scanned her face and panic spiked through her. He couldn't tell that she was in love with him. *He couldn't!*

'You look…' He hesitated.

'Stressed?' she supplied, lying madly. 'The caterers have made a mix-up with the canapés and it's made me cross. Why must these things be so hard?'

He looked as if he wanted to challenge her, but she leapt in with a question of her own. 'Has Lord Bramley signed your papers yet, the ones that will give you ownership of Ash-barrow?'

His lips twisted. 'Our estimable lord doesn't know about the papers yet. That's this coming weekend's work.'

She tried to hide the way her chest hitched. 'So you'll be back on Saturday?'

He gave a terse nod.

* * *

Will's stomach churned and he couldn't remember the last time he'd had to fight nausea
with such vehemence. He stared at the beautiful lines of Sophie's face—all smooth and
composed—and wanted to smash something.
If he hadn't been admiring her reflection in the
mirror when he'd told her he was returning to
London tomorrow, he'd have never seen it—
the stiffening of her muscles, the clutching of
that folder to her chest as if to shield herself
from some latent hurt, the dazed realisation
that had leached the light from her eyes.

If he hadn't been admiring her reflection he'd
be none the wiser. He wished to God he were
none the wiser now!

His heart pounded so hard against his ribs
it made it hard to breathe. 'Would you mind
very much if I skipped our ride this morning?
There's some work I need to get done before
tomorrow's meeting.'

'Of course not.'

She moved across and dropped a kiss to the top of his head, tossing the folder to the bed they shared, for all the world as natural and normal as if her peace hadn't been shattered.

As if her heart hadn't been broken.

His heart burned for her.

She dropped to the other side of the bed to tug on a pair of socks. A wholly reprehensible part of him wanted to reach across, undress her and drag her beneath him to slake the lust that rose through him. He didn't. He controlled the twin beasts that roared through him—lust and anger. Anger that she'd broken the rules and had fallen in love with him.

She didn't mean to!

And anger that he wasn't able to return that love.

'Gosh! I sure as heck don't want to be the person you're about to drag over the coals.'

He snapped himself back. 'Sorry, I...' He rubbed his nape. 'Work,' he growled.

She leapt up. 'Well, don't work too hard.'

With that she was gone, but Will still couldn't catch his breath or ease the constriction in his chest. He strode into the sitting room and across to the window, waited until Sophie had cantered off on Annabelle and then reached for his phone. 'Get me on a plane for London asap,' he snapped to his PA. In his head he heard Sophie berating him. 'Please,' he added.

Closing his eyes, he drew in a breath but the constriction about his chest only tightened.

Will was no closer to finding a solution to the Sophie problem on Friday night.

She'd tell him there was no problem.

But it would be a lie.

And only a coward would hide behind the lie.

He tossed his uneaten microwave meal in

the bin and collapsed to the sofa, head in his hands. For all his money and his fancy warehouse apartment, it seemed he couldn't keep the people he cared about safe—Peter, Carol Ann… Sophie. After a moment he added his grandfather to the list. The old man drove him crazy, but that didn't stop Will from caring about him.

Though both his grandfather's home and heart were safe.

He sagged back, staring at the lights that danced upon the Thames, but they did nothing to lift his spirits. 'If you were here, Peter, you'd kick my butt.' Air whistled out between his teeth, filling the silence. But nothing seemed capable of filling the chasm that yawned through him. His hands clenched. 'But I swear to you I'd rather cut off my own arm than hurt Sophie.' She deserved so much better.

She deserved the world.

He stilled as that thought pierced through him. Dear God! That was the answer, though it made everything inside him quake.

He leapt up and paced the room, back and forth in front of the windows. He'd rather hurt himself than her. He didn't *have* to hurt her. Now that he saw it, it seemed so simple.

When Will arrived at Ashbarrow the next afternoon, he chafed to get Sophie alone, except she wasn't even there.

'Last-minute wedding preparations,' his grandfather told him.

So, instead, he presented his grandfather with the legal documents that would assign Ashbarrow Castle to Will upon his marriage. To his utter disbelief, his grandfather signed them without argument. And without hesitation.

'What?' he barked when he handed the signed

document back to Will. 'It's what I'd have done in your place. There's a clause in there that states I'll have a home here until my death. That's good enough for me.'

He didn't know what to say, and then Sophie's voice sounded through him. He swallowed. 'Thank you.'

His grandfather clapped him on the shoulder. 'I only ever wanted to provide you with a home, lad. I'm sorry if I made it seem like a prison.'

He stared after the older man, had to plant his legs against the strange disorientation that battered him.

Lord Bramley turned in the doorway. 'I have no intention of interfering in your life any more, William. I'm sorry. For all of it. But you have my word from this day forward that I'll no longer try to force your hand in any way. Sophie's right, you're an adult. You've

earned the right to make your own decisions.'
He pulled in a breath before thrusting out his
jaw. 'I'm proud of you. I always have been. I
should've told you that more often.'

Will's mouth dried and he had to swallow
down a lump. 'That means a lot,' he managed.

The older man's face darkened. 'But I will
tell you this—you'll be a fool if you let that
girl slip through your fingers.'

His jaw dropped. Luckily the older man was
already striding away, a response evidently not
expected of him.

Carol Ann then co-opted him to watch, not
one, but two movies with her. He only agreed
if she promised him the second movie wasn't
a musical.

When she put on a soppy romantic comedy,
he rethought his strategy, but it was too late.
He watched the female lead's heart break and

could feel his scowl deepen and a weight press down on his chest.

Sophie came in just as the movie ended.

'Hello, Will.'

She greeted him with a kiss, composed, casual, and with her usual smile—the one that could light up a room. She was good, he had to give her that.

'Miss me?'

Her grin was full of teasing merriment. If he didn't know better…

But he did know better.

He pulled her in for the kind of kiss that sent a fire rushing through his veins. *Keep a grip.* 'Can I steal you away from your wedding prep for an hour? There're a few things I want to discuss with you.'

She glanced at her watch and grimaced. 'Will forty-five minutes do? I have the photographer coming to discuss—' she spread her hands wide '—things.'

'I'll take what I can get.'

Grabbing her hand, he raced her upstairs, slamming the door to their sitting room behind him. She gave a breathless laugh. 'You really *did* miss me.'

The come-hither blue of her eyes nearly undid him, threatened to weaken his resolve and have him tumbling them into the bedroom. Maybe this would seem more natural if they were naked and sated.

In the next moment he dismissed that idea. He'd discovered he was never more vulnerable than when he was naked and sated with Sophie.

He moved away from her. He needed space. He needed to breathe. He needed to ignore the metaphorical noose that had started to tighten about his neck.

Frown lines appeared on Sophie's brow. 'Will?'

'Something unexpected has happened.'

She perched on the edge of the sofa, those blue eyes not leaving his face. 'Your grandfather refused to sign your paperwork?'

He shook his head, still marvelling at that strange turn of events. 'Here's the thing—he signed them *without hesitation.*'

Her eyes widened and her lips parted. He ignored the hunger that roared through him when he stared at those lips.

'Not only that. He told me he was proud of me.'

Her mouth dropped open fully. She hauled it back into place a moment later. 'But that's... brilliant!'

'I know.'

'I knew he was a good guy beneath all of that bluster. I knew...'

She trailed off when he planted himself on the sofa beside her and took her hand. 'I didn't drag you up here to talk about my grandfather. Something has happened and I'm trying to find a way to tell you.'

She leaned in a little closer to stare up into his face. 'If you want to call this wedding off, Will, I'll be totally fine with that. I'll support you a hundred per cent.'

'I don't want to call off the wedding.' His heart thundered in his chest. 'In fact I find I now want this marriage to work on a whole new level.'

Her lips curved upwards. 'Sex on tap?'

He girded his loins and drew in a breath. 'I've fallen in love with you, Sophie. You've always been different from other women. I should've known what that meant.' It was easier to utter the lie than he'd thought it would be. 'I know I've always thought marriage was a…a…'

'Prison?' she offered with an arched brow.

'Exactly!' He warmed to his theme. 'I've always thought marriage would mean losing my freedom and independence, but that's not what this feels like. Not with you.'

She'd kept those blue eyes trained on his face the entire time, but now she snatched her hand from his and strode across to the window.

He moistened parched lips. 'I know it wasn't planned…that it's a shock, but… Aren't you going to say something?' He'd thought she'd have thrown herself into his arms by now, giddy with delight!

She half turned, pressing a hand to her forehead as if to keep a headache at bay. 'I'm just trying to work out how to react. Whether I ought to yell at you…'

Yell at him?

'Or whether to play along in the hope that…'

He found it suddenly hard to breathe.

'But I'll do neither.' She turned, both hands folded neatly at her waist. 'Several weeks ago I decided to turn over a new leaf—to stop hurting myself, to stop hurting others, and to become…useful. I'm not going back on that now.'

He rose, the blood pounding in his ears. 'What do you mean?'

'You've never lied to me before, Will. You don't love me. The only reason I can think for you to say you do is that you've discovered I have feelings for you.'

'Do you deny it?'

Her eyes suddenly flashed. 'No, I don't! I've no intention of lying to you the way you just lied to me. I'm not ashamed of the way I feel.'

'But—'

'I didn't mean for it to happen, but it has. You've always meant a lot to me. You did before Peter died…and you've come to mean more to me since.' She rolled her eyes. 'Evidently.'

'Then why not—?'

'I don't want to trap you into a marriage you don't want. That's not love! What kind of person do you think I am?' Her hands slammed to her hips. 'And I'm a little offended you think I can't cope with having a broken heart. I'll survive, you know? It'll mend in time.'

'But—'

'No.' She held up a hand. 'The original plan stands. We marry and you get to safeguard Carol Ann's future while I get a million pounds. We spend the wedding night here at Ashbarrow Castle and then the next day you're for London and I'm for Cornwall.'

'But—'

'No buts. And no more sex. It's obviously addled your brain.' She glanced at her watch.

'I'm sorry, you'll have to excuse me. I have to meet with the photographer now.'

He watched her go and wondered why, when she'd just let him off the hook, his world felt in ruins.

CHAPTER TEN

SOPHIE DIDN'T SEE Will all week. She hadn't minced her words when she'd told him that she hadn't wanted to see him—that if he really wanted to help rather than hurt her, he'd keep their contact to a minimum for the foreseeable future.

She didn't spend her nights sobbing into her pillow. She spent them staring up at the ceiling and calling herself every kind of fool she could think of for not getting with the programme and pretending to believe him when he'd told her he loved her.

But everything inside her rebelled at the thought of trapping him into a pretence of love and commitment. A fake marriage was one thing, but to pretend it was a true union—soul mates, hearts and flowers, promises of forever—was something else entirely.

In the darkness, she shook her head. She tried to find a measure of comfort in the fact that he'd not have attempted to make such a sacrifice if he didn't really care for her, that he'd not have made it for any other woman, but in reality it was a cold comfort. He might care for her, but he didn't love her.

She tried not to ache for the life she wanted with him, but it was impossible not to. All she could do to keep herself strong was remind herself how such a marriage would leave him feeling suffocated and trapped. How, in the end, he would come to hate her.

And *that* she couldn't bear.

She knew she had to stay strong because on Saturday—the day of the wedding—she suspected Will would try again. He hadn't got to where he was by giving up.

The day of the wedding, a morning in early October, dawned clear with an invigorating chill in the air. Sophie slipped out of the castle and down to the stables to saddle Annabelle. Today of all days she needed to ride—needed to calm her nerves, to quieten the clamour of her mind, so she could present a picture of calm composure to the world in a few hours' time.

Will was waiting for her on her return. Her stomach softened at the sight of him, but she straightened her already straight spine. He'd stayed at the pub in the village last night…but he looked haggard, as if he hadn't slept a wink.

She swung down off Annabelle. 'I thought it was bad luck to see the bride on the day of the wedding.'

'I'm thinking it's only bad luck if she doesn't show up to the church.'

He tried to smile, but it didn't really work, and it was all she could do not to hug him. She handed Annabelle's reins to the stable hand who magically appeared. 'Is everything okay?'

'No. Everything is wrong.'

She led him to a bench in the kitchen garden bathed in early morning light and scented with rosemary and lemon balm. 'Tell me. I'm the party planner extraordinaire, which translates into me being an expert troubleshooter. Has the best man broken his leg? Have half the guests come down with food poisoning? Hit me with it, Will. I'm used to dealing with last-minute emergencies.'

He jutted out his chin and glared. 'I love you, and you refuse to believe me. *That's* what's wrong.'

She swallowed. She hadn't expected him to sound so...*sure*. He must've been practising.

'Last week when I told you I loved you I didn't realise it was true. I said it because—' he flung an arm out '—because I didn't want to hurt you, because you deserve to be happy, because you deserve the best. But my whole week has been grey and bleak and miserable.' He raked both hands back through his hair. 'I've felt as if I've been stumbling through a thick fog or...or trying to wade through quick-drying cement. I've been an idiot, Sophie, a grade-A fool.' He hauled in a breath, resting his elbows on his knees, looking so haggard her stomach started to churn. 'I told myself to pretend to love you because the truth scared the living daylights out of me. What good is my so-called independence and freedom if I don't have you? I love—'

'Stop it!' Her voice came out sharper than

she meant it to, but his every word was a cold stab to her heart and she couldn't bear any more. 'That's enough. I know you feel guilty, but you've no right to toy with my affections like this.' She shot to her feet, trembling with the power of emotion coursing through her, from the strength it took to hold back from throwing herself into his arms. 'If you really respected me, *cared* for me, you'd stop this now.'

'But—'

'This is not the time for such a discussion!'

He shot to his feet too. 'It's the day of our wedding! What better time is there?'

'A wedding for a paper marriage, a fake marriage, Will. That's the arrangement and that's what's happening here today. You have no right to change the rules now.'

He took her shoulders in both his hands, his eyes blazing down into hers. 'Even if the real thing—a marriage based on love and respect—would add greatly to both our happiness?'

He looked so convincing she wanted to slap him. 'Maybe I have misjudged you. Maybe what you want is more important to you than what I want? Maybe easing your guilt is more important to you than my need for space?'

He took a step back, his face white. His hands dropped to his sides. 'I only want you to be happy. I only want what's best for you.'

'Fine! Then rather than forcing your version of happiness onto me, let me make the choice for myself.'

He stared at her for a long moment and then nodded. 'This isn't over.'

Whatever. She turned and started for the house. 'I'll see you at the church.'

Three hours later Sophie stared at her reflection in the full-length mirror that had been brought to her suite of rooms and gave a satisfied nod. She looked suitably bridal. She'd chosen a wedding gown in a nineteen-twenties style—a dress with a slim skirt, but overlaid with lace and intricate beadwork. Those who knew her well would smile when they realised the dress wasn't white or cream or ivory or dove grey, but the palest shade of pink.

Carol Ann stared at her from the other side of the room, where she was doing her best not to crumple her own gown. 'You're the beautifullest woman in the world, Sophie,' she breathed in awe.

'We're the most beautiful women in the world,' she corrected. Carol Ann looked a picture in her pale lilac dress. 'Okay, you better help me on with my veil.' A heavy Chantilly lace and chiffon number that would hopefully hide the strain in her face when she made her farcical vows to Will.

Once her veil was in place and she clutched her rather splendid bouquet of peonies, she sent Carol Ann a smile—if it trembled she doubted anyone would notice. 'Ready?'

Carol Ann nodded vigorously.

They made their way down the stairs to find Lord Bramley and her father waiting in the great hall. Both men turned to watch her descent. Lord Bramley grabbed a large handkerchief from his trouser pocket and blew his nose loudly. 'You look a picture, my dear, a perfect picture. Don't you agree, Collingford?'

'Lovely,' her father agreed, and for a moment she fancied she saw approbation in his eyes. 'I'd kiss you, but…' He made a vague gesture in the air.

She nodded. 'It's probably best that you don't muss me up.' Her heart started to pound and she feigned preoccupation with her skirt. 'It's nice to see you here, Father. I take it you spoke to Mother and that she's waiting at the church?'

He stiffened. 'Absolutely not! I thought I made myself more than clear on that front. I vowed to never speak to that woman again and I've no intention of ever going back on my word.'

She nodded, her heart burned but she refused to let her chin drop. 'Very well. I believe I also made myself clear on that particular point. Your assistance at this wedding will not be required. Lord Bramley—' she turned to the other man '—would you be so kind as to walk me down the aisle?'

Lord Bramley's mouth worked as he stared from one to the other. He snapped his mouth closed and gave a hard nod. 'I'd be honoured and delighted.'

'You can't do this,' her father roared at her. 'I'll be a laughing stock!' He paused to draw in a breath and the sudden silence pulsed with fifteen years of unspoken things. His hands clenched to fists. 'You promised to never choose her over me.' The words were quiet but deadly.

Sophie lifted her chin. 'It's a fine thing to hold your child to ransom over a promise made when she was eleven years old! When she had no real idea of its consequences. And, just for the record, I'm not choosing her over you. I've spoken to her, yes, but she said she'd only come if she had your blessing.'

He gave a harsh bark of laughter. 'Because otherwise she knows she'll lose the house in Spain and the money I settled on her as part of our divorce agreement. Rethink this decision, Sophie, or understand that I'll never forgive you.'

Neither one of them loved her enough. Had it always been that way? 'I've not chosen her over you,' she repeated. 'I'm asking you to choose me over your hate.'

He blinked.

'Your pride and desire for revenge are still more important to you than your daughter's happiness *on her wedding day*.' She frowned. 'Doesn't that shame you?'

He opened his mouth. He closed it again.

'I refuse to be a pawn in your nasty little game any longer. If you want to be a part of my life and the lives of any children I might have, then you need to change. I won't bar you from the church, and I won't throw you out of the reception, but until you contact Mother and build a bridge there, all contact between us stops.'

'But—'

'No buts. I'm tired of men trying to bully me and direct my life. I'll steer my own course, thank you very much.' She took Lord Bramley's arm and started for the door. She turned back just before they stepped through it. 'You've lost one of your children through no fault of your own. You have a choice with me. This time it's up to you.'

'Are you sure about this?' Lord Bramley said when the limousine pulled away from the castle grounds and towards the village abbey.

She turned to meet his gaze. 'About what? Not having my father walk me down the aisle? About marrying Will?'

'Your father.'

She nodded. 'Oh, yes, I'm sure about that. Sad but sure.'

He blew out a gusty breath. 'Your father always was a frightful prig. I hope he comes to see sense, my dear.'

So did she.

He sent her a calculating look. 'What would you have done if I'd refused to take his place?'

Her lips twisted. 'Don't take this the wrong way, Lord Bramley, but to be perfectly honest I'd prefer to walk down the aisle on my own and give myself away—I'm nobody's property or responsibility. But it'd cause a stir, and you know how much Will hates that kind of thing. So...'

He stared at her for several long moments. 'The boy loves you, you know.'

'So he says,' she said, grateful when they pulled up in front of the church.

She breathed in a cleansing breath as she stepped out of the suddenly cramped confines of the car, but Lord Bramley followed right behind her. 'But you don't believe him?' he persisted.

She bit her lip and took another breath, before turning to face him. 'How can I believe it when this is a marriage you've forced him into? He's marrying me because he must.'

There seemed no harm in saying so now—not after he'd signed Will's papers.

Her conscience pricked her though when he seemed to age before her eyes. She forced a smile to frozen lips. 'But never mind. I expect we'll muddle along.'

'I wanted so much more for him. I'd like so much more for you too, lass.'

Tears blurred her vision, and she found herself gripping his hand hard. 'If that's the case then go in there and tell him he doesn't need to marry, that Ashbarrow is his and Carol Ann will always have a home there.' He had the power to stop them from going through with this awful farce of a wedding.

He patted her hand, his eyes damp. 'I would, my dear, except I promised the lad I'd no longer interfere. I gave him my word. Believe it or not, I've finally learned my lesson.'

She gave a shaky laugh. 'Finally the man develops a conscience.'

'I only ever meant well.'

'I know.' She squeezed his hand and kept her mouth shut about the road to hell being paved with good intentions. She wasn't going to hell. At the end of this day she'd be a million pounds richer. Well, actually, nine hundred thousand pounds richer, seeing as though she'd had that advance, but it was more than enough to build a new life for herself. And for Carla if the other woman wanted to be a part of it.

It was enough.

It would have to be enough.

The church was full. It seemed the entire village had turned out to watch Will marry. A sigh went up when Sophie appeared at the end of the aisle. A chorus of nose-blowing ensued, which normally would've made her smile. However, while she might present the picture of a perfect blushing bride, she couldn't smile. She could focus on nothing but the man waiting for her at the end of the aisle.

The man she loved with every atom of her being.

The man she was going to marry.

The man who was breaking her heart.

He looked stunning, which was no less than she deserved, she decided. If her heart had to be broken, she wanted it broken by the best.

Those dark, dark eyes matched the black of his tuxedo; the stark white of his dress shirt highlighted the colour mounted high on his cheekbones, softened only by the pale pink rose in his buttonhole. He stood tall and firm and solid. She stiffened her spine and pushed her shoulders back, determined to match him in every way, determined not to let him down.

They'd go through with this pretence of a

wedding. And then tomorrow she'd let him go with courage and grace. When some time had passed she'd make sure they salvaged their friendship. And then everything could go back to being the way it had always been.

Liar. Nothing will ever be the same again.

Need, desire, possessiveness all roared through Will the moment Sophie appeared at the end of the aisle. But as she slowly made her way towards him, it was quickly followed by despair. He loved her. He loved her in a way he'd not realised it was possible to love another person. He loved her in a way that didn't frighten him. She'd never try and tear him apart the way his parents had tormented and persecuted each other. Having Sophie at his side wouldn't make him weaker. It would make him invincible!

But she didn't believe him. And he didn't know how to convince her that the vows he was about to make to her were vows he ached to make, that he'd mean them with every fibre of his being.

You have time. Not today, but tomorrow and the day after.

He had the rest of his life to convince her that he meant what he said—that he loved her. And he would convince her. Somehow.

It was only when the minister asked, 'Who gives this woman to be married to this man?' that he realised it was his grandfather and not Lord Collingford who had walked her down the aisle. The burning glare his grandfather sent him made him swallow.

'You look stunning,' he murmured to her as he took her hand. He wanted to pull her to one side and ask her if she was all right, to find out if her father had upset her.

He couldn't. It would be outrageous, would cause all sorts of gossip and speculation.

'Ready?' the minister said.

Sophie turned back to the front. 'Absolutely.'

That was when Will saw it—the silvery track of a single tear making its way down her cheek. He turned to face the minister too, his throat thickening.

'Dearly beloved...' The minister started the service.

What the hell was he asking her to do? This must be tearing her up inside.

Tomorrow. You can make this all up to her tomorrow.

Or better still, he could make it up to her to-night. Or, even better, right after the ceremony. He would prove to her that he was sincere.

Yeah, right, like you managed that so brilliantly this morning.

He closed his eyes as the minister droned through the introduction to the ceremony.

'If any of you can show just cause why they

may not lawfully be married, speak now; or else for ever hold your peace.'

His eyes sprang open and he found himself holding his breath.

Sophie glanced at his grandfather, who refused to meet her gaze. Will's lungs started to burn, but his grandfather remained seated. Sophie's shoulders slumped as she turned back to the front, and Will couldn't stand it any longer. He opened his mouth. He snapped it shut again.

Deal with it later. Don't make a scene.

He glanced at Sophie. He wished he could see her face behind that damn veil better.

What if later is too late?

'Damn it!'

The minister's head rocked back at Will's curse. 'Mr Trent-Paterson?'

'Sorry,' he muttered, but, honestly, if there was ever a time to make a spectacle of himself it was now. Sophie was worth it. She was worth everything.

He released her hand. 'I have a reason why we shouldn't marry. The bride doesn't believe I love her, and I can't have her marry me when she's operating under such a misapprehension.'

Sophie's gasp filled the hushed church. 'Will,' she whispered. 'The press are here.'

'I don't care.'

'You will tomorrow,' she whispered back.

'Come tomorrow I'll know whether I've won or lost you. Tomorrow nothing else will matter to me except that.'

Her mouth worked, but no sound came out. Eventually she turned to the minister. 'Reverend Todd, do you mind if Will and I retire to your vestry for a moment?'

'Not at all.'

For a moment Will was tempted, but then he planted his feet and remained firm.

'Will,' she groaned. 'You hate public scenes.'

'I do. But we're staying here. If it'll help you realise I'm serious then I'm willing to risk one.'

Her every muscle suddenly twanged with tension. She seemed to vibrate with it. 'Now I'm mad!' she ground out.

Mad was better than martyred. He pointed to her veil. 'You could be anything at all behind that thing and I wouldn't have a clue. I can barely see your face.'

Her hands clenched to fists and she swung back to the minister. 'Reverend Todd, would you be so kind as to give me a hand with my veil?'

'It's most improper. I—'

He broke off at whatever Sophie managed to convey to him beneath the folds of lace. Even Will saw the blue flash of her eyes and they weren't currently focused on him.

'Of course, my dear Ms Mitchell.'

When she swung back to him, her entire face was alive with fire and frustration. The breath caught in his throat even as a smile curved his lips. Now *this* was his Sophie.

She flung an arm out to encompass the congregation. 'How do you think this is going to convince me of anything?'

She'd been trying so hard to reform her image, to stay out of the papers, and here he was flinging her right back into the middle of all that again. He understood her anger.

But he knew exactly what he had to do. It should frighten him witless, but it didn't. The only thing that frightened him now was losing Sophie. He couldn't bear to think of his life without her in it.

'I love you, Sophie.'

She glanced away, lips pressed tightly together.

'And I think I've finally found the way to prove it to you.'

She glanced back, her chin tilted at a defiant angle while her eyes blazed blue outrage at him. It took all the strength he had not to pull her into his arms and kiss her. She wouldn't accept the physical as a symbol of the emotional. Not yet.

He wanted—needed—her to come to him instead.

Very slowly he drew out the document from the inside pocket of his morning suit. Unfolding it, he held it out for her to see what it was.

She glanced at him with suddenly unsteady eyes. 'That's the agreement between you and your grandfather.' She took it and scanned it, before handing it back with a shrug. 'There's nothing new here—no clauses I was unaware of.'

Without another word he tore it in half. Her

eyes widened and she tried to grab it, but he evaded her to tear it in half again.

'Will, don't be an idiot!'

He tore it again and again…until it was nothing but black and white confetti. He flung the pieces into the air.

She watched them flutter to the ground, mouth agape. 'What are you doing?' She stared at him. 'Have you lost your mind?'

'Finally—*finally*—I'm seeing things clearly. I refuse to buy a home for me and Carol Ann at the expense of your happiness.'

She stared at him with uncertain eyes. 'This isn't necessary.'

'I think it is. If my grandfather makes good on his threats I'll find a way to cope with the fallout. You've shown me that's possible. You've shown me what I'm capable of. What I'm not capable of is living without you.'

She swallowed and he wondered if she realised that she'd edged a step closer to peer up into his face. The hope she tried to hide nearly tore him in two.

He'd made so many mistakes—mistakes that had hurt her—but he'd make them up to her a hundred times over if only she'd let him.

'You *never* wanted to marry.'

He nodded, but not in agreement. 'I never understood the power of love before. I didn't understand it until this week. And you know what?' It was his turn to thrust out his jaw.

'What?' she whispered.

'Not every marriage is as detrimental and destructive as my parents' marriage. Or your parents' marriage either.'

She nodded. '*I* know that.'

'I'm *not* my father.' He thumped a hand to his chest. 'And you're not my mother.'

Tears shimmered in her eyes, making them

look like a bright summer morning filled with promise. 'You love me?'

He nodded. 'With all that I am, with everything I have, with my entire heart.'

He pulled forth another document—the contract he and she had signed. He held it out to her. 'Tear it up, Soph.'

She stared at it. She stared at him. She folded her arms. 'You need proof of my love?'

No! But this was in effect a pre-nuptial agreement, which entitled her to nothing other than that million pounds. He wanted to give her everything, not just a measly million pounds!

Her laugh suddenly rang around the church—merry and full of joy. He'd not known if he'd ever hear it again. Hope he'd barely dared to entertain threatened to lift him off his feet. 'Sophie?'

She took the contract and slid it back into his

pocket. 'Not a chance, Will. I don't want your money. I don't need your money.'

'But—'

'Will, I only want you.'

And then she took his face in her hands and pressed her lips to his in a kiss so full of warmth and promise and love that it nearly knocked him off his feet, but then she pulled away to fling her arms about his neck, and holding her righted him again. It righted the whole world.

'I love you, Will. I'm not sure we have any right to be so happy after playing such foolish games, but I love you.'

He took her face in his hands. 'I want to marry you for real, Sophie. I want to love, honour and cherish you,' he murmured, his heart pounding in anticipation for what he planned to do with her the moment they were finally alone. 'Forsaking all others,' he added. He wanted them very clear on that.

She nodded. 'Yes, please.'

'So...' Reverend Todd broke in. 'Does this mean you wish me to continue with the service?'

'Oh, yes, please.' Sophie turned with shining eyes. 'We're definitely getting married today.'

Behind her the entire congregation cheered. Will was too happy to groan. 'From the top, if you please, Reverend.'

'Dearly beloved...'

EPILOGUE

'WE HAVE MADE so much money for Peter's charity!' Sophie said over the music, and Will smiled at the way her eyes danced, the way her excitement brought her entire face alive. She squeezed his hand. 'Isn't that the most wonderful news?'

He brushed his lips across her cheek. 'It is. And I'd be happy to donate more. I—'

She dropped his hand to point a finger at him, doing her best to look stern but failing miserably. 'You've given more than enough, thank you very much.'

'You've pulled off an amazing event.' He slid an arm about her shoulders and pulled her in close, burying his face in her hair for a moment to fill his lungs with the scent of her, relishing the way she pressed against him. *This*—having Sophie close—made everything right. *Everything.* The joy, the exhilaration, the contentment, none of it had waned in the sixteen months they'd been married. He delighted in making her happy. He delighted in her.

He glanced down into perfect blue eyes—giving thanks as he did every day—and then nodded across the glittering ballroom filled with smiling beautiful people towards her parents. 'Who'd have thought we'd live to see this day?'

Her mouth opened and closed and she gave a dazed shake of her head. 'I still can't believe that they're not only speaking, but also actually working together. I know you're behind this, you know?'

'Not true. It was your father's determination to make things right with you coupled with your mother's immediate acceptance of the olive branch he proffered that set this in motion.'

After Will and Sophie had returned from their honeymoon, Lord Collingford had contacted Will begging to know how he could make things right with his daughter. Will had merely suggested that he and Sophie's mother might consider working together to create a lasting memorial to Peter. The older man had immediately run with the idea. Hence, the establishment of the Peter Mitchell Foundation.

When her parents had presented the idea to Sophie she'd offered her services as an event planner immediately, and with a grace that had humbled Will. Her capacity for forgiveness and desire to make things better inspired him. The Peter Mitchell Foundation raised funds for medical supplies for Third World countries. It seemed a fitting memorial to a man who'd been so passionate about the cause.

'Now...' He turned Sophie to face him.

'What was Mildred Campbell talking to you about so earnestly?' He'd watched from the other side of the room, intrigued at the play of surprise, interest and delight that had flitted across Sophie's face at the time. Mildred was the owner of Moreland Park Equestrian Centre—the one he'd taken Sophie to see that first week she'd been stuck at Ashbarrow. He hadn't known Mildred would be here tonight.

'Oh, now this is exciting! She wants us to go into business together. She's been watching how well my equestrian holiday packages in Cornwall have been doing and wants me to create something along similar lines in Scotland. She's offered me a partnership.'

His jaw dropped. 'That's brilliant news!'

He shouldn't be surprised. Sophie deserved her success. She and Carla had been working tirelessly to get the stables in Cornwall up and running. In addition, Sophie had brought her event-planning skills to the fore in the holiday packages she'd started offering. In and of themselves such packages weren't unusual, but Sophie's mix of eclectic evening entertainments to complement the daytime riding—streamlined to meet each tour group's requirements—had proved a runaway hit.

She glanced up at him. 'You really think so?'

'Absolutely! Mildred's a tough cookie. Rumour has it she drives a hard bargain, and she doesn't suffer fools gladly.' He recognised a fellow entrepreneur when he saw one. 'The fact she's offered you a partnership—in her beloved equestrian centre, no less—is proof of her respect for what you've achieved. Heck, her hard-headed business acumen coupled with your creativity…' He shook his head. 'You'll have taken over the world before we know it.'

She leaned back to stare into his face, twisting a lock of hair about her finger as she surveyed him. 'Well, I'm glad to hear you're so supportive of the idea, because...'

'Because?'

He tried to look hard-headed and shrewd, but her smile told him she wasn't fooled. 'Because if I decide to take up the partnership it'd mean spending a lot of time in Scotland. Like, perhaps, six months of the year.'

Sophie could have whatever she wanted. He meant to make it his life's work to keep her happy. He'd move to the North Pole if it was what she wanted. As far as he could tell, there wasn't a single reason why they couldn't move to Scotland. Pyxis Tech didn't need him—he'd put a capable management team in place. He was free to go wherever he wanted.

He glanced around the room until he found Carla, who was talking with a group of other women. 'You think Carla is ready to take over Cornwall on her own?'

'More than ready.'

Something in her voice had him swinging back. 'Have there been problems?'

She shook her head. 'I just mean Carla's already in charge of the daily running of the stables. And I know she's grateful to me...'

'But?' he asked softly.

'It's time she started dating again.'

Ah. 'And you think that could be awkward for her with you around?'

She grimaced. 'Don't you?'

He chewed his lip for a moment. 'Will you be okay with it when she does meet someone?'

She nodded so eagerly her hair bounced. 'I can't wait for that to happen. I want her to be as happy as we are.'

He should've known that would be her answer.

'And I know she's grateful to me for everything, but I'm sure she must feel like I'm watching her—to make sure she doesn't slip up. I'm not, but…' She shrugged. 'It's just time to let her take over the reins in Cornwall completely.'

'While you conquer new horizons in Scotland?'

'Exactly.'

He pretended to scowl. 'Well, I'm not living in Ashbarrow Castle.'

Her mouth dropped open. 'Will! You and your grandfather are getting on great these days.'

They were, although the older man still liked to get a rise out of Will whenever he could. They still argued about everything from estate management to politics. He was here somewhere. Will scanned the room, and, while he spotted Carol Ann on the dance floor, he couldn't see his grandfather. He'd probably snuck out for a game of cards with a few other like-minded souls.

'True,' he allowed. 'But it doesn't mean I want to live with him. And I also love it when Carol Ann comes to stay with us in London or Cornwall, but...'

'But?'

He slipped his arms about her waist and drew her in close, relishing the way her breath hitched as their bodies met. 'But I'm not ready to share you with anyone just yet. Not full-time.' He loved the freedom of kissing her whenever he wanted, of making love with her whenever they wanted. He wasn't ready to have their hours-long conversations inter-rupted or cut short by other people. He wasn't ready to relinquish their privacy. 'How does a little cottage somewhere not too far from Ash-barrow sound?'

She stood on tiptoe, her lips a breath's distance from his, and things inside him clenched up tight with need and heat. 'Will you be there, Will?'

He nodded.

'Then it sounds perfect.'

Before he could answer, she feathered a kiss across his lips in just the way she knew drove him insane. The heat in his blood spiked, his skin suddenly feeling too small for his body. He captured her face in his hands before she could draw away and deepened the kiss in the precise way he knew drove her insane, trailing his tongue along the inside seam of her lower lip with a slow precision until a ripple of desire shook through her body.

They were both breathing hard when they eased apart. Their love hadn't waned and nor had their desire. He revelled in that knowledge.

She smoothed down her hair and cleared her

throat. 'By the way, did I mention I'd booked us a suite here for the night?'

Heat sped through his veins and he didn't bother trying to tamp down on the desire coursing through him. 'You didn't.' His London apartment was only fifteen minutes away, but… 'So, if you were to leave the party early?'

She glanced at her watch. 'Ooh, I think the event planner clocked off about two minutes ago.'

He needed no further encouragement. Taking her hand, he made straight for the exit. Sophie started to laugh, but she didn't resist. 'So there's nobody you want to say goodnight to, then?'

'Only my wife. But I can assure you it won't be because I'm wishing her a good night's sleep.'

She arched an eyebrow at him, but he could see the pulse fluttering in her throat and he couldn't wait to place his lips there, to lathe it with his tongue. 'I do intend her, however, to have a good night. A *very* good night.'

Wordlessly, she collected their key.

They waited with another couple for the elevator. When the other couple exited at the third floor and they had the space to themselves Will wasted no time in backing Sophie up against the far wall, and beginning a sensual assault on her throat, pressing kisses there, grazing the skin lightly with his teeth until she clung to him.

'If you don't stop that,' she murmured, her voice gratifyingly breathy, 'you're going to have to carry me because my knees are in danger of giving way.'

The door to the elevator pinged open, and in answer he swept Sophie up in his arms and headed for the door at the end of the corridor.

'Will?'

He slowed at her softly whispered question, meeting her gaze.

'I love you,' she whispered, her eyes the bluest of blues.

His gut clenched up tight.

'I love you more than any equestrian centre, or event-planning business, or…or anything. If you'd rather not move to Scotland, I truly wouldn't mind. I just want you. If I have you then nothing else matters.'

He stared down at her and his heart grew so big he wondered how his chest could contain it. 'Sophie, I have everything I want right here in my arms. Where we live doesn't matter to me as long as you're there. I love you. I have no right to be this happy.'

Her smile was like his sun. 'You deserve every bit of happiness that comes your way,' she told him. 'And I promise that in about two minutes' time you're going to be even happier.'

With low laughs, and promises of love forever, they fell into their room and set about proving exactly how much they treasured each other.

* * * * *